I0570856

Totally Bound Publishing books by Tina Donahue

Taming the Beast
Freeing the Beast
Surrendering to the Beast
Mastering the Beast
Muzzling the Beast
Disciplining the Beast
Seducing the Beast

Taming the Beast

SURRENDERING TO THE BEAST

TINA DONAHUE

Surrendering to the Beast
ISBN # 978-1-83943-809-7
©Copyright Tina Donahue 2018
Cover Art by Posh Gosh ©Copyright April 2018
Interior text design by Claire Siemaszkiewicz
Totally Bound Publishing

SURRENDERING
TO THE BEAST

Dedication

To Tina's Romance Rebels, my awesome street team. And to my PA, Pamela Leonhardt. Ladies, you have made this journey so worthwhile.

Chapter One

Heather clasped her hands to her chest, lowered her head and tried to believe as she never had before. "You can do this, you can do this, you *can* do this."

Her personal mantra, gained from countless self-improvement books, online courses and seminars she'd attended. The writers and sponsors always promised the programs would make her a new woman in business, life and love.

As a good fairy, that wasn't likely, but she needed all the help she could get. Born to be kind, patient, sympathetic to a fault and purer than the driven snow, she simply wasn't assertive enough during work hours or on the dating scene. Not that she'd ever tried to hook up with guys. Even thinking about talking to one in a romantic sense made her dizzy enough to pass out. Since none had flocked to her on their own, especially the shy ones who'd prove non-threatening, she was lonely and wanting.

That left her career to fill the endless hours where her innate personality still got in the way. Always, she feared hurting someone's feelings no matter the consequences to herself, her BFFs or the business where she and they worked.

Serving as the receptionist and healer at From Crud to Stud, a New Orleans makeover service for supernatural beings, was a monumental undertaking. She had an honor-bound duty to make certain the clients left there healthy and hearty, that their appointments were up-to-date and that they never stiffed the service on money they owed. Being an overdue bill collector was the hardest part of her job description.

But it had to be done. Right now. She'd delayed too long on this account and only had herself to blame.

Nausea rolled through her as she steeled herself to do battle with Satan. To her horror, her Skype call to him connected instantly. Her vision dimmed but she faced her webcam and his image on her computer monitor.

This evening, he resembled a European playboy, a cognac snifter in one hand. He'd slicked back his dark hair and wore a blood-red ascot that contrasted nicely with his white shirt and navy blazer.

For a bad guy, he certainly knew how to dress.

"*Cara mia*." Heat smoldered in his voice and dark eyes. "What can I do to you?"

She wanted to hurl but gave him her sternest look. "I'm sorry, I don't mean to correct you, but I think you meant *for* me not *to* me." He never got the phrase right.

Grinning, he focused on her white peasant blouse and jutted nipples, her areolas tightened from the chilly weather, not him. Tonight was damp and cool, thanks to a spring storm that raged in the French Quarter. Lightning flashed. The office lights flickered. Just like in a slasher film.

Flames flared briefly in his pupils.

They didn't calm her apprehension.

He leaned closer to the screen, his eyes boring into her. "We'll do many things to each other, no?"

Heather would have given anything to flee but pretended she hadn't heard his vulgar question. A knee-jerk reaction for someone with her genetic makeup. Needing to get tough, she held up his overdue bill and hoped he'd look at it rather than her chest. Her hand shook so badly the paper rattled.

"How you tremble," he cooed. "How pale you are. Allow me to put some color in your lovely cheeks. Heat that will last an eternity."

Her skin grew clammy. "Please, just pay your account." She waved the paper and prayed she wouldn't lose her nerve. "Your grandson failed to show for his last two appointments. I'm sure he had a good reason. Unfortunately, he didn't call to cancel. Because you're the cardholder, we had to charge you for the time. I'm so sorry, really I am, but it is the rule."

One she was obligated to enforce to keep this place solvent and humming. In the treatment rooms, vampires hissed, weres howled and demons snarled obscenities. She cringed at that awful language but understood their pain and the others' agony, too. These poor souls suffered proverbial hell to suppress their beasts so they could date mortal women without freaking them out, while also winning their hearts the normal way. With real charm, not magic. With integrity and love, not lies and manipulation.

Those miracle transformations didn't come easily or cheap. They took the staff's valuable time and clients needed to pay for the effort. Even Satan should understand such a simple and fair concept.

He offered an indulgent look. "What charges?"

His bill burst into flames.

Heather gasped and dropped the paper in her trashcan.

"Later." He killed the call.

She smothered the small blaze and chided herself for not having been firm with Satan's grandson when he'd signed up for the service. Determined to make up for being too nice, she brought up her bank account to pay the charges herself. After that, she'd book a spot at another assertiveness training workshop. One had to do the trick for her. Clinging to that hope, she filled in the required spaces on her online payment form.

The lights flickered twice, thunder boomed and the front door flew open.

It banged against the wall.

She flinched.

Dank air and rain blew inside, followed by a guy who looked to be thirty or so. He wore a black cowboy hat, snug navy tee, low-slung jeans and cowboy boots.

He shoved the door shut, slumped against it and breathed hard.

Heather shot to her feet. Her chair rolled into the numerous potted plants behind her.

He didn't notice. His eyes were closed, face raised to the ceiling. His prominent Adam's apple bobbed from his hard swallow.

Although alarmed at his entrance and who he might be, she was also intrigued. Something that had never happened before when it came to a guy who might not be a customer here. On those occasions, she'd always hurried in the opposite direction.

Her legs refused to move.

Short, dark hairs dusted his throat. Rain dampened his cocoa-colored hair. Those thick, wavy tresses flowed to his broad shoulders that heaved with his ragged breaths. Tall, six-three or so, he was nicely muscular.

Virility she found protective rather than daunting.

His wet tee clung to his well-defined pecs and abs, those bruising biceps. His bronze skin betrayed an outdoorsy nature rather than a guy who spent his days working indoors.

His scent wafted toward her. A fresh and woodsy fragrance, along with an unmistakable beer or wine odor.

Her panic flared. It wasn't often that mortals, drunk or otherwise, happened upon this place. When they did, she had ironclad rules to follow. First, buzz Constance, her BFF who was also a voodoo priestess. Given Constance's power, she could remove memories by laying her hands on someone's head. A necessary evil so the mortal world would never know what went on within these walls. Following that, Heather was supposed to notify Becca, also her BFF, and a half-mortal witch who owned this place.

She leaned over her desk to press the intercom button.

The guy turned to her, blinked and stared.

His eyes were amazing, the color of Lipton tea, ringed by long, sooty lashes, his attention riveted as he drank her in. Given his slow, sexy smile, Heather suspected he undressed her with his eyes.

Her skin burned worse than it had when she'd faced Satan, yet this heat felt good, like comfort and excitement combined. She hadn't a clue why that would be and didn't have time to figure it out. She needed to get the others up here.

He groaned mournfully.

The agonized sound surprised her. Her empathetic nature kicked up several notches. "Are you all right?"

"Fuck, no," he panted. "These pissing boots are killing me."

They were as masculine as him, the tooled black leather sporting thick silver buckles. Although they weren't refined or gentlemanly, she liked them. Now, his language...

"I gotta sit down." He lurched to her desk.

"No. Please." She held out her hand to stop him. "Go back outside and —"

An ear-shattering howl ripped through the office. Roaring thunder followed. The were wailed away.

He stared at the hall and the treatment rooms beyond.

Too late now for him to waltz out of here with his memories intact. Heather felt bad about that but had to do the right thing for her friends and the service. "Let me get Constance."

His legs bowed. "I need to take a load off." He eyed her chair.

She raced toward him without thinking, desperate to block him from commandeering a seat. Her forehead barely reached his shoulder and he also outweighed her by ninety pounds or better, but she couldn't let him see anything on her computer screen. It would expose the business even more than the were's outburst had. If this guy left before Constance removed his memories... Heather didn't want to consider the possible exorcisms and purges that would follow.

The people who worked here were her family — the only real one she had. To protect them, she'd become more than assertive with him, she'd get rude, maybe even mean. She struggled to frown.

He staggered back to the door. Propped against it, he pulled off his right boot. It clunked on the faux-brick floor. His left boot followed.

Air hissed through his teeth.

Heather pressed her hand to her chest. She'd expected to see his socks, maybe even his bare feet, not hooves. "You're not mortal."

"No kidding." He puffed out another breath. "That's why I'm here." He gestured to the reception area stuffed with potted plants and feathery ferns. The greenery made the coral walls seem even warmer in comparison. Faux-gas fixtures provided a dated, romantic feel, like old New Orleans.

Loud hisses and teeth snapping filled the hall.

He arched one dark eyebrow and raked his gaze over her.

Perspiration rolled down her back and between her breasts.

Pleasure sparkled in his beautiful eyes. "I take it I'm in the right place for a makeover?"

Few beings had deeper voices than his. Awe blossomed within her. A pleasant feeling. Her nipples tightened. She liked that, too, when she shouldn't have. Given the huge bulge behind his fly, she guessed what he was. "You're a satyr, right?"

"That's me. Wine, women and song." He winked.

A zombie moaned.

He looked over. "Speaking of song, you should get a sound system in here. Drown out those crappy noises with some down-and-dirty heavy metal. You like Behemoth? Their *Lucifer* kicks serious ass."

His bulge got bigger, the folds between her legs damper. Fighting dizziness, Heather plodded to her computer, mystified as to why he had such an enticing effect on her when other guys had only sparked panic. Satyrs were charming, sure, and natural seducers. They had to be, considering all they thought about and wanted was sex. However, they didn't have the power to turn a good fairy against her ingrained principles. At least, she didn't think they could. "Do you have an appointment, Mister…"

"No Mister, just Daemon. Nope on the appointment, too. I'm hoping you can fit me in. What are you?"

Heather stopped keying. "The receptionist."

He laughed with pleasure, not derision.

The deep, virile sound rushed straight past her bones and into her marrow. Her belly fluttered.

"I mean what kind of being are you? No, wait. Let me guess." He tapped his forefinger against his bristly jaw.

He wore an ornate silver ring with a large black stone on his right middle finger. His hands were big and rugged rather than frightening.

Heather wasn't certain why, but she saw good strength in them, the sort that cherished and made mortal women sigh in appreciation.

She might have whimpered in delight, but didn't have enough breath.

He made a frustrated sound. "You're either an elf or a fairy. Damn, I can never tell those two beings apart."

That hurt deep. Fairies and elves weren't similar at all. No different from mistaking a satyr for a centaur. Despite his rude comment, she couldn't be surly or sarcastic. "I'm a good fairy."

"That explains all the white you're wearing." He gestured to her peasant blouse, gypsy skirt and ballet flats.

An outfit she'd bought at Macy's, not a uniform store for fairies. Heather knew she wasn't cool like the babes he probably knew and had been intimate with, but he didn't have to make her feel like a total loser. Embarrassed, she lowered her face. "I like the color. It suits me."

"Hey, I'm not arguing." He held out his hands in surrender. "I'm all about pleasing the ladies." He grinned.

His teeth were white and straight, his smile raffish yet charming.

Heather shook off her arousal. "I'm sure you are and you haven't." She hit the computer keys harder than usual and checked the appointment book. "Zoe can see to you in twenty minutes." Zoe, another BFF, was a reformed demon who knew how to keep guys from getting too frisky. "Please grab your boots and follow me."

He clopped after her and stopped abruptly to read the business name and its motto, *Suppressing the Beast*, painted on the wall. He shook his head. "Damn shame what we guys have to go through now to snag the babes."

"You mean mortal women." His biceps were beyond awesome, beefy and firm. Prominent veins coursed down them. "I understand nymphs are still into satyrs."

"True, but I want to try the other side." He planted one hand on his flat belly and swiveled his hips. "Boogying in a bar or nightclub rather than Couturie."

Technically, Couturie Forest, a sixty-acre woodland within the city and a popular recreational spot for mortals. To supernatural beings the area was also a known habitat for satyrs and nymphs. So far, humans hadn't a clue what went on in the vegetation.

Daemon leaned toward her. "Tourists are getting downright intrusive. Know what I mean?"

Unfortunately, she did but that was the price satyrs and nymphs had to pay if they frolicked nude. Heather struggled not to peek at his groin. "What exactly did you want us to do to you?"

"Make me one hundred percent human-looking on the outside."

"Oh." She hadn't expected that. "You don't want an attitude adjustment to go along with the other stuff?"

He focused on her breasts to the exclusion of everything else. "Something wrong with my attitude? What's your name, by the way?"

"Heather. I don't mean to be rude, but my face is up here." She pointed.

Daemon didn't bother to look. His handsome features flushed. Carnal hunger filled his eyes. "I want the whole enchilada. New legs, feet, get rid of the tail, my horns."

No wonder he wore a hat.

"Use magic or cut the stuff off, stick new stuff on, I don't care. Do what you have to. If things go wrong, so what? I heard this place has a healer."

She should have fessed up about her special talent but couldn't get her mouth to work.

Daemon edged closer.

His wonderful scent surrounded her.

He lowered his mouth to her ear. "Would that healer be you? Will you be tending me if anything goes wrong?"

If Heather had to touch his various body parts, she wasn't certain she'd be able to stop. Denial to his question was on her lips, but she wasn't able to speak the words. Good fairies couldn't lie. "I will."

"Awesome." Raw power and heat radiated from him.

She trembled and ordered herself to step away. "Let's see what we can do."

Once inside the evaluation room, she filled in the form with his name and goal—to be fully human physically so he could boogie with mortal babes and not a good fairy. She left the last part off. Not that it mattered. Her penmanship was too sloppy to read, her hands shaking more from him than they had with Satan. His put-on seduction had scared her witless. Daemon's was natural and far too arousing.

She pushed her feelings aside. "Before anyone can give you a treatment here, I have to ask you some questions. I'm sorry, but those are the rules. Please answer truthfully, so there aren't any complications."

"You mean problems? What kind? Oh, hey, my cock won't get soft, will it? Jesus, are my balls going to shrivel? That would totally suck." He paced, or rather clopped, across the room. "If that happens, you will be able to make me better, right? I mean, do what you have to. Touch me, rub me, take me in your mouth. Whatever puts me back to the way I was."

Her legs wobbled. She leaned against the counter for support. "Ah…" She cleared her throat. "Every client who leaves here is whole. We make certain of that."

"Thank God." He released a huge sigh. "So are there ever good complications?"

"What do you mean?"

"Maybe unintended consequences is a better way to say it. You know, my rod getting longer and harder. I'm not complaining about the way I am now, but hell, I wouldn't mind an extra inch or two."

Heather wiped sweat from her neck. "I can't be absolutely certain, since I don't do treatments, but I think the only things you have to worry about are your hooves, tail and horns. We really should begin. Are you allergic to anything?"

"Do cowboy boots count?"

She held back a smile. "I'm sorry about your poor hooves. It must have been awful to have to walk here."

"Hey, one more mile and I would have been sobbing like a disgraced politician. Ow. Damn."

He dropped his hat on the floor. Bloody stumps protruded from his hair.

She pulled in a breath. "What happened to your horns?"

"Broke those suckers off."

"Why?"

"To get the stupid hat on." He touched a stump and winced. "It's not as bad as it looks."

She ached to heal him but had to get through the paperwork first then secure his payment. Shivering, she returned to her form. "Have you had any major illnesses?"

"Nope." His tee sailed past her and landed on the counter.

An inexplicable urge to press her face to his shirt hit her hard. She couldn't think of anything except taking in his sublime scent, pure freshness mixed with musk.

Something rustled and fell to the floor.

Heather guessed his jeans and forced herself to concentrate on her questions. "Are you currently taking any magic potions?"

"Just wine. I'd kill for a zombie, though—the alcoholic kind—or a boilermaker."

After checking *no*, she read, "Has anyone cast a spell on you within the last six months that altered you significantly before you went back to your original form?"

"Not unless a wish is like a spell, which I hope it's not," he muttered beneath his breath. "Let's just say if I'd gotten what I'd wanted, rather than what I asked for, from MJ—who knows better and should do better when it comes to pleasing a Master—I wouldn't be here. You can save the questions. I'm spell-free and healthy as a horse. No different from when I was born, except bigger."

"I have to ask." Heather wondered who MJ was and what he'd meant about pleasing a Master. She turned and stilled.

He was less than a yard away and nude, gloriously so. His pecs were smooth and hard, his tiny nipples the same color as damp earth. His abs were so defined they could have been carved from stone. Silky dark hair trickled beneath his navel to his hairy groin. Rooted in those curls was his…uh…his…uh…

Cock.

The indecent term rose unbidden in her mind, possibly because Becca and Constance used the word when they talked about guys. Heather finally understood why. Nothing else could describe how ungodly thick his shaft was. Probably a foot long and rigid. Ready to party.

Her mouth went dry. She should have fled but didn't, preferring to ogle his lightly furred balls. Another obscene word from Constance and Becca that described his sac so well.

His long tail was silky like one on a horse, but also prehensile like those on monkeys. It snaked around his thigh and made a beeline for her.

She needed to back away but couldn't. "What are you doing?"

"Sorry. My damn tail has a mind of its own." He slapped it down. It jumped right back up and zipped toward her again. "See?"

His tail wrapped around her waist and reeled Heather in, smack against his solid chest. She froze. The damp clothes had left him slightly chilled. Miraculously, his skin grew hotter by the second. Hers did, too. His thickened rod brushed her thigh and lengthened an additional inch or more.

Uh-oh. She ordered herself to fight whatever was happening. Nothing on her moved except her thoughts. *You should pull away. Now. Right now. This is so wrong. This is —*

She sagged into him, unable to resist. Gold flecks brightened his irises. His heat and powerful form made the world go away. "What?"

He stared at her.

She did the same with him. "Huh?"

"I didn't say anything." He touched his nose to hers. "Did you?"

Answering wasn't something she could manage. Every word she'd known went bye-bye.

"Okay." He fitted his mouth to hers.

Heather forgot how to breathe.

His lips were unspeakably soft, his breath hot and scented with liquor, his caress gentle but so wrong. They didn't know each other. They'd barely met, if she could call it that.

She parted her lips to say something, anything, maybe even to thank him for such a wonderful yet immoral moment.

Daemon slipped his tongue inside her mouth, his kiss wet, searching and shameless, straight from the Dark Side.

Her skin tingled and her toes curled. Breathtaking feelings she'd never known and couldn't have predicted whizzed through her. Whether they were supposed to or not wasn't something she could answer. She had zip experience with mortal or immortal men. Even her thoughts were always pure.

No more.

His tongue tasted better than any food she'd ever eaten. His masculine scent and everything else about him thrilled her, even though it shouldn't.

Because it did, she enjoyed him.

Her mouth was wonderfully loose beneath his, her kiss not tentative or virginal as Daemon had expected. Not that he had boundless experience with untried maidens. When he'd been young and clueless, the older nymphs had set him firmly on the right path, running him down and crawling all over him until he submitted.

He hadn't fought hard. Before those babes could blink, he'd plunged his rigid cock into their succulent flesh. The younger nymphs had watched, and when it was his turn to test and tame their innocent flesh, they'd been as skilled as him. A real bummer for a guy who needed a thrill from the chase and a conquest.

He slanted his mouth for greater penetration and deepened his kiss.

Like a real trooper, Heather wreathed her arms around his neck and sucked his tongue as if she'd been born for the task.

Fuck, life just doesn't get better than this. She was the first good fairy he'd tasted, and damn, was she ever luscious, a combination of something minty, possibly toothpaste or candy, and something far better and ethereal. Similar to perfume from a flower carried on a morning breeze, the taste only a raindrop can offer and soothing heat as sun caresses the Earth.

Best of all, she smelled powdery, pure and sweet.

He filled her mouth as much as he could and wanted to rip off her dainty clothes, get down to business and forget the fucking foreplay or being a nice guy. In Couturie, one look from him and a nymph would assume the position, so to speak. Or she'd blindside him and they'd roll across the forest floor with her taking whatever she wanted.

That kind of raw lust had nothing to do with sweetness and charm.

Heather was so gentle and soft Daemon throbbed from need. He pulled her closer.

She stiffened, made a wounded animal noise and pushed against his shoulders.

His lust punched up several degrees. He cupped her small breast and thumbed her nipple.

Heather tore her mouth from his and gasped. "Stop."

He didn't want to but dropped his hand, thinking the challenge would make this even hotter. *Nope.* Now, he was frustrated. "Why?"

"We're strangers." Her breath skipped across his chest, making his skin tingle. "We don't even know each other's last names."

"I don't have one." He itched to squeeze her breast again. "Do you?"

"Well, no, but—stop."

"Sure." He cupped her ass rather than her boob.

She sighed lustily and trembled. "That's not much better."

Maybe not for her, but gripping her rounded butt did wicked things to his cock. The damn thing was so fucking hard his skin was about to split.

She stroked his chest. "Let go of my…uh…my… Please."

That last word and her quivery voice undid him. Like a good boy, he behaved as she wanted and ran his knuckles down her velvety cheek instead.

Heather lifted her face to his. Her eyes were a fragile green softened by gray, her waist-length hair moonlight pale, the locks silky and thick, her gaze filled with too much honesty and trust.

He could have done without that. "Better?"

"Well, no. I liked what you were doing, but it's wrong." Embarrassment pinched her pretty features. "So thanks for not doing it any longer."

"Ah, sure. Anything for you."

She regarded him with wonder.

He couldn't do anything less with her.

They were back to staring at each other. Felt good somehow. "What?"

She blinked slowly and brushed her lips over his.

He stopped breathing.

She did, too.

Before he could close his eyes, Heather pushed her tongue into his mouth.

If Daemon could have found enough air, he would have groaned and growled to convey the heat burning within him, his hunger for her and his appreciation that she was back on track, ready to get physical. They turned in tight circles, each trying to get closer. His hooves clomped on the tile. Her slippers slapped delicately.

Thunder boomed, rattling the window. Something let out a blood-curdling shriek. The door in here flew open.

"Oh, hell, no." A female made a pissed noise, her voice so guttural the sounds vibrated in his belly. "Get your hands off her."

Heather pulled back.

Daemon looked over.

A thin young woman with black hair, flames in her eyes and metal studs in her face grabbed his tail and twisted it hard.

White-hot pain tore through him.

Heather flapped her hands. "No, no, no."

His thoughts exactly.

His attacker rammed her saddle shoe into his sore hoof.

Agony ripped through him. His life flashed before his eyes. The details weren't pretty.

Heather whimpered. "Zoe, no."

She growled. "On the table." Without giving him a chance to comply, she rammed her shoulder against him.

He lost his balance. His nuts hit the furniture. Everything went shrieking white then blood red. He yowled.

"Quiet." In fast order, Zoe had him on the treatment table, his wrists and hooves strapped so tightly the leather dug into his flesh. Breathing hard, she smoothed her demure white blouse and green plaid skirt. Smoke rose from her shoulders and hair. "Not a sound from you. Understand?" She spoke to Heather. "How many times have I told you to wait for me before you bring a new client into a room for treatment?"

"It wasn't his fault. His tail has a mind of its own."

Zoe regarded it. "Is that right? Let's see what it thinks about this." She yanked.

The pain shot every-fucking-where, even to his teeth and eyelashes. Daemon bellowed and fought his restraints.

"Stop." Heather sandwiched herself between the she-devil and him. "I didn't call you because of his stubs — horns — what used to be his horns. He needs a healer."

"If he doesn't behave, he'll need a reaper." Zoe crossed her arms and glared at him. "Make one move, say one word, *please.* I'll be happy to take you out."

Daemon wrinkled his nose. Not only was her attitude beyond shitty, she smelled awful, like burnt matches. "Is this the way you treat all your customers?"

She pushed her face into his. "Only those who attack staff members."

"He wasn't attacking me." Heather bounced on her heels. "He's not a bad guy."

Well, yeah, he was. Daemon felt guilty for lying to her about his wayward tail and not wanting to stop when she'd insisted upon it. Hardest thing he'd ever done. Pure fucking hell that had thickened his blood and done wonderful things to the junk between his legs.

In Couturie, sex had become so predictable and ordinary that he merely went through the motions with nymphs and even MJ, who was another story entirely. His climaxes were so-so, not earth-shattering. They frustrated rather than fed his inner need for more and had ultimately brought him here. He'd heard mortal women could be bitchy as hell about sex and demanded endless shit before putting out. For someone who'd always had a willing female at his disposal, trouble beforehand sounded intriguing, maybe even fun.

Like kissing Heather. That had been great.

For the first time in forever, excitement rather than boredom sang in his blood. What a treat it would be to have Heather beneath him, her milky skin flushed with color, lips bruised from his kisses, nipples tight from his mouth, her cunt wet and wanting as she willingly sheltered his cock.

If being a good boy was what it took to get that, damn right he'd give it a shot. No pain, no gain.

Zoe eyed him suspiciously and pulled on the straps, cutting off his circulation.

Chapter Two

Constance, Becca and Zoe congregated in the treatment room.

Heather stood to the side, forgotten and ignored, as always. Those training courses called to her now more than ever. If only she brimmed with aggressiveness, she could be in here alone with Daemon.

Her limbs grew weak. Her spirit yearned. That was beyond wrong, but somehow, she didn't care. Fat lot of good it did her.

Becca paged through a new witchcraft primer she called 'magic for dummies'. She'd just purchased it from a pop-up ad on her laptop that came on after her spell had tanked. Being a lousy witch, she'd needed her mom's help when Eric, a descendant of Cupid, had come to the service to release his beast rather than suppress it. The first potion had messed things up pretty bad, but everything had turned out well since Becca and Eric lived together now.

Zoe's history wasn't as happy. A long-ago tragic love had soured her on guys, so she'd sworn off them and sex and kept everything strictly business. She leaned against the door and reviewed the thick contract clients had to sign before anyone did anything.

Constance wasn't needed at all. She'd breezed in a few minutes ago, looking like a high-fashion model, with her gorgeous ebony skin and outfit—a fuchsia gown and matching turban. She circled the treatment table and zeroed in on Daemon's balls and cock. No one would ever accuse her of being shy around guys.

Heather blamed herself for how things had turned out tonight. No one had thought she could handle this or anything else because she was always too nice. Resolved to prove them wrong, she recalled the assertiveness exercises she'd studied and spoke up. "I appreciate your help, really I do, but all of you have your own work. I can manage this alone."

Becca pushed her flame-red hair behind her ear and flipped another page. Zoe ran her finger down the contract and mouthed what she read. Constance inched closer to Daemon.

Heather screwed up her face and courage. "Will everyone just go?" No one responded. "Please?"

They didn't budge.

Daemon gave Heather a sympathetic smile.

Her legs went watery.

Constance bent over his groin for a better look.

He regarded her good-naturedly. "Doing okay there? Anything I can do to make your viewing experience more pleasurable?"

She giggled. "Sorry, but damn, you're one amazing guy. I gotta get this on my smartphone." She wagged a bejeweled finger at him. "Don't you move."

As if he could, given how Zoe had strapped him in. "That's enough." Heather squared her shoulders to Constance and everyone else.

They didn't notice.

Fine with her. She concentrated on Daemon.

"Whoa." Zoe grabbed Heather's wrist before she could touch his restraints. "What are you doing?"

"His hands and the skin above his hooves are turning red from lack of circulation. I need to loosen the straps before they hurt him."

"Even if they do, you can heal whatever's messed up." She shrugged. "We'll add the new charges to his account."

"That's not nice."

Zoe frowned. "It's business. Wait. Don't anyone move."

Wind slammed into the window, punctuating her command. Rain hammered the glass.

Constance had already stopped at the door.

Becca rested one hip against the counter. "What's wrong?"

Zoe jabbed her thumb at Daemon. "Does Romeo have the dough for this?"

Heather hoped he did. If she kept paying for clients who stiffed them, she'd go broke.

Daemon gave her a heated smile that turned icy for Zoe. "Check my jeans front pocket."

She pulled out enough cash to choke an elephant. The flames in her eyes danced.

Constance offered a thumbs-up. "Looks like he's raring to go. Be right back. Don't start without me." She slipped out of the door.

Zoe stopped counting the bills. "Are these real?"

Becca craned her neck to see. "Better hold them up to the light. They should have security strips."

"Wait." Heather didn't like this one bit. "You've practically accused him of not being honest. I thought we were better than that. I thought we were here to help and comfort."

"We are. Soon as we get paid." Zoe scanned each bill, nodded and stuffed them in her skirt pocket. "We're good. I don't want to know if he stole this."

"Zoe." Heather tapped her foot. "That's mean."

"Wrong. It. Is. Business."

"Ladies." Daemon winked at Heather and gave Zoe a sour look. "For your information, I didn't have to steal the money or anything else, for that matter. I have my sources."

"I'll bet." She lifted the contract. "You need to sign this before we can do anything to you."

"*To* me, not *for* me? And don't I get to read the contract first?"

"Nope."

Heather pulled the papers from Zoe and held them behind her back "I'll read it to him. I don't mind."

Smoke belched from Zoe's shoulders and hair, proving how irritated she was.

Becca spoke to Daemon. "Before we do anything, we need to know if you want the change to be permanent or not."

"Hell, yeah. Wait." He looked thoughtful. "Define permanent."

Becca ran her fingers over the tiny amethyst stars dangling from her navel jewelry. The color matched her silk top, harem pants and lipstick. "Anything that needs more magic to turn you back to the way you are now."

Zoe chimed in, "If you choose that, there's an added cost."

"Does there have to be?" Heather leaned closer to her and Becca. "Can't we give him a discount?"

Becca shook her head. "Sorry, but if we did that, we'd have to take it out of your pay."

At this rate, she'd never build up a nest egg. She spoke to Daemon. "I'm sorry, really I am, but you need to be sure."

"What the hell. Let's go for broke."

Zoe pulled a pen from her skirt pocket and slapped it on the treatment table near his bound wrist. "Signature and initials first."

"No." Heather laid the contract and pen on the counter. "I'm going to heal his stubs before anyone does anything. He's in pain."

Daemon moaned.

She suppressed a smile at his lousy acting and pleaded with Becca. "Please. I need to heal his poor hooves, too."

The cowboy boots had scraped the skin above them raw. A gross yellowish liquid oozed from the wounds.

"You can do your thing in a sec." Becca regarded him. "You need to understand something before we begin."

"Don't worry, Heather already asked me if I'm allergic to anything. I'm not. Except maybe to her." He wrinkled his nose at Zoe.

She bared her teeth.

"Everyone chill." Becca rubbed her temple. "There are things about the treatment that would make an allergy seem like a trip to Disneyland."

He leaned away as much as he could, given his restraints. "Like what?"

"There's going to be a shitload of pain once we start, and I'm not talking about getting rid of your stubs or tail. That's relatively easy. The potion we have to use for your legs and hooves dissolves them, after which—"

"What?" Heather gasped. "Are you sure? Maybe we should ask your mom for one of her spells."

Zoe mumbled beneath her breath. Sounded like "good idea".

Becca made a face. "It's all in here." She stabbed her finger into the book. "There's no easy way to get new legs and feet." She spoke to Daemon. "You ever read *The Little Mermaid* by Hans Christian Andersen?"

He frowned. "The little what by hans who?"

Heather didn't understand. "Why are you asking him about that?"

"It's a cautionary tale. About changing yourself and the pain—not pleasure—that follows. Be careful what you wish for and all that." Becca spoke to him. "Something to consider before you do anything to change yourself."

"No, it isn't. I've already done what you've said. No way am I putting my well-being into MJ's hands again. That would be pure lunacy."

It was the second time he'd mentioned those initials. Heather was too curious to pretend otherwise. "MJ?"

"Don't you worry, I've got it covered." He lifted his right hand as well as he could and curled his fingers except for the middle one which he extended.

Heather wasn't certain if he was flipping her the bird for prying into his personal business or if he meant to show off his ring. Hoping for the latter, she nodded. "Maybe I should google the tale so we know what to expect before we begin. If the back-cover copy doesn't tell us enough, we can order the book."

Zoe chimed in, "Only if he pays for it."

"With what? You have all my cash." He turned to Becca. "I'm no masochist but I'm definitely onboard with doing this. Any chance I can get something to take the edge off, like a zombie?"

"The alcoholic kind." Heather remembered everything he'd said and had done. Especially their kiss. A depraved yet spectacular moment. "Right?"

Tenderness filled his face. "You nailed it."

She blushed.

Becca pushed her bangs off her forehead. "I'll see what I can do about the booze. We'll give you the treatment in the morning. See you then."

"Wait." Heather clasped Becca's wrist as gently as she could and eased her across the room to keep him and Zoe from overhearing. "Can Daemon stay here tonight? I wouldn't ask, but if he has to walk back to Couturie and here again, his hooves are going to be bloody stumps." She sagged. "I'm sorry for being so forward about this, but I don't want to see him hurt."

"I know you don't, sweetie." Becca patted her arm. "But I can't let you unstrap him. Someone, probably you, would have to stay here to make certain nothing bad happens, like him chewing through the restraints, getting loose and attacking you again. You see the problem?"

"He didn't attack me. And I don't mind staying here. I can read him the contract."

"It's a real snoozer. It'll probably put you to sleep."

"Him, too. That wouldn't be bad. Please?"

Becca looked doubtful but nodded. "You call Zoe ASAP if you need help, got it?"

She'd always ask for assistance if things tanked. It was the sensible and right thing to do. "I promise."

"Let's go." Becca led the way out. Zoe didn't move. Becca blocked Constance from entering. "We're leaving Heather and Daemon alone."

"Seriously? I don't think so. How about I protect her?" Constance lifted her smartphone. "While I do I can take shots of his—"

"No, you can't. Go back to work. Now." Becca shooed her away and gestured to Zoe. "You, too. Out."

She mumbled obscenities but departed. Smoke trailed after her.

Becca shot Heather a warning look. "Be good." She closed the door.

A weary howl floated down the hall. In its wake were tired hisses and groans. Everyone seemed to be beat. Even the rain had calmed to a gentle shower that should have soothed.

Heather had never felt more alive.

Daemon's welcoming smile drew her closer, the moth to the proverbial flame. Her feelings were reckless but she couldn't seem to stop them, didn't want to. For the first time in her life, she wasn't controlled or afraid. Being uncivilized rocked. No wonder everyone else indulged themselves. Heedlessly and wantonly, she stroked the matted hair around his left stub, taking care not to hurt him.

Daemon fought his restraints to reach her.

"Easy." She rested her hip against the table so he could touch her waist. Even that was pushing the envelope. She didn't care.

His fingers dipped lower to her hip.

A throaty moan bubbled up. She shoved it back down and curbed her lust. "Daemon."

Behaving himself, he stroked her skirt waistband. "You amaze me."

"Because I try to be good?"

"Shit, no. You really kicked ass with your coworkers."

Heather's cheeks burned at his foul yet kind words. "No, I didn't. I'm too nice. Surely, you've noticed." His roaming fingers must have. She eased them from her butt to her waist.

Innocence and tenderness shone in his eyes. "You're fine as you are."

She teared up at his sweet sentiment. "So are you. Why do you want to suffer through all this just to go to a bar or a nightclub?"

Daemon shrugged. "It's complicated."

He didn't want to tell her and she couldn't be rude and pry. "Let's take care of this."

Gently, she traced his left stub. The ragged edge scraped her fingers and tore at her heart. No one should have to go through agony, whether it was from magic, plastic surgery or whatever, so others would accept them. It wasn't right, but it was the way the world worked.

Beneath her healing touch, the edges smoothed and the blood disappeared. "Better?"

His chest expanded with his deep breath. "Fuck, yeah."

Heather shook her head at his language but didn't scold. Now wasn't the time. She leaned closer and stroked his right stub, healing it.

Daemon's hand fell away from her hip, his fingers curled gently. If he'd had feet, she'd bet he would have splayed his toes.

She smiled, wanting warmth and comfort to replace his hurt. Not only because she'd been born to feel as she did, but because she genuinely liked him. He might have had nothing on his mind except booze and sex, like most mortal guys, but she sensed he also had a good core. A giving heart that wouldn't allow him to harm anyone deliberately and a sweet nature behind his male bravado.

No one, not even him, could convince her otherwise. He was a good guy.

She loosened the straps on his wrists and ran her forefinger beneath the leather to ease whatever discomfort he felt.

He breathed peacefully.

The raw skin above his hooves was gruesome. She bit her lip to keep from crying out. With the lightest touch, she healed those wounds, loosened the straps and ran her fingertips over his leg for good measure.

He growled lustily. His cock grew thicker and longer.

There wasn't anything she wanted to watch more, but couldn't. That would be wrong. After grabbing the contract, she pulled a chair over. Close enough for him to hear her, yet far enough away to keep him from getting any ideas. Her, either.

Daemon arched an eyebrow, but he didn't complain.

Seated, she read quietly, detailing his obligation to pay in full for add-on treatments before additional work commenced, and how he couldn't hold the service responsible for anything that went wrong.

Talk about boring shit. Halfway through the second page, Daemon couldn't keep his eyes open. His lids sagged, the insides gritty from sleep.

"Provision number five." Heather cleared her throat. "The customer, still known as Daemon—no last name given—a satyr currently residing in Couturie Forest, will hold the aforementioned service blameless in the event of..."

He drifted off, Heather's breathy voice lulling him, her words no longer registering. *Pattering rain commanded his attention. The forest and his hidden lair flashed in his mind. Its woodland scent filled him, along with a powdery fragrance.*

Heather's.

Daemon smiled. In his dream, he reached for her.

She slapped his hand. "Don't touch my ass."

Right. One of her good fairy rules. Hoping there weren't too many more, he grabbed her skirt to haul her in as a gentleman would. She sighed disapprovingly at that and the muddy smears he left on her, but she didn't resist. They rolled over the rain-drenched leaves and moss, and tore at her clothes. Daemon ripped them away faster than she could.

Bared to him and the heavy moon, Heather nearly glowed, she was that pale. Except for her pinkish nipples and the plump folds between her legs. He pushed her down to the thick grass and spread her thighs, prepared to feast on her slick pussy.

She grabbed his stubs and wrenched his head up, keeping him from pleasure.

"What's wrong? I didn't come anywhere near your ass."

"I know. But you need to remember the little what."

He'd never forgotten it. However, no one had ever called his cock that, not even when he'd been an infant. "I'm not correcting you…okay, I am. It's not little." *He flexed his rod.*

She put her knee on it. "Listen to me."

At this point, he had no choice. "Sure."

"I'm talking about the cautionary tale. The one you didn't read. The book you won't pay for. Do you want this to be permanent?"

If she meant her endless talking then no. He ached to get down and dirty. He pulled her feet from the mud and propped them on his shoulders. "Let's take care of business."

Before she could object, he licked her cleft.

She squealed.

Liking the sound, he tongued her clit.

Her bawdy moans rippled through the vegetation. She was fire in his arms, writhing, panting and wailing out her climax.

He was far less civilized, the noises he made neither human nor animal but a combination befitting ageless carnal need and raw lust that made the world go round. He settled between her legs, ran his cock up her damp pussy and lifted his face to hers.

Zoe, not Heather, stared back at him.

He woke with a start, drenched in sweat, heart pounding.

Heather stood at the counter, her back to him as she emptied three large sacks.

Awesome bread and meat odors bombarded his senses. His belly growled.

She looked over and smiled. "Good morning."

By God, it was. Watery sun streamed past the closed shutters, bathing her in its gentle rays. She'd changed from her white top and skirt to a different white top, this one with a high collar and full-length sleeves, and a long white skirt. The hem touched her toes.

For some reason, he pictured her feet covered in mud. Something inside him fluttered. Her smile made him rock hard.

Heather stared at his cock. She even took a step toward it before shaking her head and backing away. "Are you hungry?"

He could have feasted on her for days and wanted nothing else, which was saying a lot since he was always starving. Not that he was crazy enough to voice his lewd thoughts given her uptight belief system and that she had to be talking about food. "Sure."

"I googled what satyrs eat. You're an omnivore."

"Cool."

She laughed, a tinkling sound, light as a baby's sigh.

It did more for him than an orgy at a BDSM club. His rod stiffened beyond belief and his balls ached. "Did I say something funny?"

"Oh, no. I wasn't laughing at you. I'm sorry if you thought that." She pressed her hand to her chest. "An omnivore means someone who eats plants and animals."

The bags she'd rummaged through looked to be from Mickey D's. So did the wrapped packages and Styrofoam containers on the counter. Could be he was wrong about what they held. "You foraged and hunted this morning?"

"What? No. I couldn't hurt any kind of animal. I don't even know where they are, except for dogs and cats that roam around. Those I usually feed, which kind of brings more here. At that point, Becca calls a no-kill shelter. She's a good woman. As to this…" She gestured to the counter. "I went to McDonald's and got several of everything on their breakfast menu so you could have your pick and fill."

She placed the wrapped sandwiches between his legs.

Daemon lifted his head as well as he could until his neck and shoulders screamed in protest. He fell back and grunted. "I can't reach them from here. Shove as many of them as you can in my mouth." He opened it wide.

She looked appalled. "How about I unstrap your wrists so you can eat like you normally do?"

"You're sure? Zoe might come back." His balls still sported black-and-blue bruises from her.

Heather waved away his worry. "She's rumbling with a warlock. It'll be our secret."

What do you know? The good fairy had a dark side. "You're actually going to do something bad?"

Panic swept across her face. She shook it off. "If you eat lying down, you could choke to death. That would be bad."

He couldn't argue the point. "Thanks."

The second he was free, he rubbed his wrists and fought a depraved urge to grab her for some hard loving.

She peeled away the paper on each sandwich then pointed to the junk stuffed between the buns on the first one. "What we have here is really good. My personal fave. It has—"

"Let me stop you right there. I know what McDonald's serves."

"You've been there?"

"No. Tourists have. Sometimes they leave their stuff in the forest without finishing it. They lose things, too. Cell phones. Tablets. Do you have any of the McGriddles?"

She handed him one with sausage, egg and cheese.

He licked her thumb, as a gentleman would. Just as he'd seen an actor do in a black-and-white movie playing on an android. A mortal had lost the thing in Couturie, which was great. Unfortunately, the stupid device had gone dead before the flick ended. Maybe they had a smartphone here he could play with. He'd heard about *Avatar* and was dying to see it. "Thanks." He gave her a sweet smile and shoved the entire sandwich into his mouth.

Her eyes goggled. "No, wait."

Daemon spoke around the food. "You changed your mind? You want this back? Give me a sec and I'll spit it out."

"No, don't, please. Keep it." She shuddered. "On the next one, though, you should take smaller bites, like this." She showed him.

At that rate, he'd starve to death, but didn't quarrel. Following her lead, he plowed through the fare at a glacial pace until she turned away to get the drinks. He shoved a sausage biscuit and an Egg McMuffin into his mouth then swallowed hard. Chewing would only slow things.

"Coffee or milk?" She held up both.

A Busch or a Coors would have been nice. He belched and pointed to the coffee.

She handed him the cup and took a seat. "I'm not being critical, but you're not supposed to make noises like that, either."

He stopped sipping the hot coffee. "You want me to lap it with my tongue?"

"No. I meant burp. You shouldn't do that."

Great, another rule. "Why?"

"Mortal women don't like it."

He'd forgotten about them and why he was here, willing to have his hooves and legs dissolved in order to grow new ones so he could boogie at clubs and bars. Places he figured Heather never went to, for reasons other than being a good fairy.

His curiosity about her grew, crowding out his desire to be with mortal babes. "You still live with your folks?"

She stopped lifting a sausage burrito to her mouth. "I never lived with my birth parents. I was adopted."

"By mortals?" He considered the worst and made a face. "Conservatives? Damn. Wait." There was no getting around how prudish Heather was, except when she cut loose. For a split second. Then it was back to her puritanical ways. He finally understood why. "Ultraconservatives? Freaking fundamentalists?"

"Oh, no, by…other fairies."

Her hesitation interested him. "They weren't good like you?"

She slumped. "Let's just say they liked to skirt the rules. I wanted to understand their reasoning and I'm sure they wanted to know what made me tick, but we didn't get along that well."

"You actually rebelled against them?"

What little color she had drained away. "No, never, even though I came close to disagreeing once." Her mouth turned down. "That was so awful, it haunted me for weeks. I did try to explain why I wouldn't harass mortals, or steal or do anything illegal, and how sorry I was for failing them, but they got fed up with me. I kind of had to move out and get my own place."

"And a job here?"

"That came first." She beamed. "Becca's my BFF. She saved me from the streets. I didn't have any money and hadn't eaten in days when she saw me outside McDonald's. I was too scared to go inside and ask for a job. I didn't have any references or skills to speak of for them to even consider me. Becca bought me three Quarter Pounders and offered me a job here. I really owe her for giving me a chance and teaching me so much. Do your parents live near you?"

He chuckled. "Are you kidding?" Forgetting himself, he shoved two cinnamon melts into his mouth and spoke around the sweet treats. "Once a male satyr comes of age, his old man kicks him out of the community." After swallowing, Daemon made certain not to belch. Wasn't easy, but for her, he'd be a gentleman. He scratched his armpit and groin. "Dear old Dad wanted the young babes for himself. Can't blame him. That's the way things go. I set off on my own and ended up in Couturie after I fought the head dude there. He ripped me good." He pointed out the scars on his forearm. "Long story short, I held my ground and told him it was my turf now whether he liked it or not."

"That's awful."

His grin faded. "Why? If I hadn't beat his ass and staked my claim, I would've still been homeless like you were."

"That's not what I'm talking about. It's terrible that your parents would kick you out."

He shrugged. "Shit happens. Look at what those SOBs did to you."

"They were confused...*are* confused."

"Ah, hon, they're pricks. Trust me on that one."

She straightened. "Is that why you want to change, so someone will finally love you?"

He leaned away from her. If Zoe hadn't strapped him down, he probably would have run. "No. I'm looking for a good time — a different kind of good time than I'm used to." *The thrill of the chase.*

Heather shook her head. The way a woman does when she doesn't agree with a guy or doesn't believe him. "You shouldn't change for anyone. You're perfect as you are. They should accept you that way."

He imagined clopping into a popular watering hole, stubs exposed, his tail swinging while he tried to score with the babes. It wasn't a pretty picture. "If I don't change, I'll be stuck in that forest or one like it forever." *Dodging mortals, eating their leftovers, never seeing the end of movies, screwing around for the sake of screwing around.* "There has to be more."

The door swung open.

In slogged Becca, her arms filled with containers and bottles Daemon guessed held stuff she'd use to make her potions.

Chapter Three

Heather worried and paced.

Becca measured and stirred.

Daemon wolfed down his breakfast faster than he had earlier. Heather guessed he thought this would be his last meal ever.

After Becca added the final ingredient to the bowl, she regarded the sickly green mixture and sniffed. Her face turned the same shade as the concoction. Hurriedly, she dumped it out, swallowed hard and started fresh. That witches' brew lasted even less time before it ended up in the sink. She heaved in a deep breath and looked over. "I know you don't trust me to do this right."

Unable to lie, Heather said the only thing she could. "I know you'll do your best."

Becca muttered an obscenity, shoved her hair behind her ears and got down to business. Several tries later, the newest potion was finished, its center a sickly gray. The edges glowed bright green and brown. She checked it against the photo in her book and nodded.

Daemon belched.

Heather didn't have the heart to scold. Having to drink the potion was punishment enough for him. It even smelled bad, kind of like Zoe.

"Now for his zombie." Becca trudged to the door. "Be right back."

Heather waited until Becca's footfalls had faded. Wasting no time, she pulled her smartphone from her purse.

Daemon shoved two Egg McMuffins into his mouth. His cheeks puffed out from the food. "You going to watch a movie? I hear *Avatar* is legendary."

"What? No." She couldn't catch her breath.

"Everything all right?"

"Ah… Remember, small bites." She turned her back to him and made her call.

Rowena, Becca's mom, picked up on the second ring. "Heather?"

"Yeah, hi." She kept her voice low so Daemon couldn't overhear. "Sorry to bother you this early. I wouldn't ordinarily, I hope you know that. I realize you're probably still eating breakfast, and it's rude of me to interrupt you when you—"

"It's okay, sweetie. What did Becca do?"

"Nothing yet." Heather cocked her head, alert to Becca's return. No footfalls sounded in the hall. Not that it was quiet by any means.

Zoe and a warlock rumbled in the room across the way, both snarling threats at each other, with hers being the loudest. "I said get on that damn table or else."

The warlock barked a laugh. "Or else what? You think someone as puny as you could make me do anything? I'll blast you from here to the ends of the—"

A crash sounded, followed by a screech several octaves higher than the warlock's usual timbre.

Heather cupped her hand over her phone and mouth. "Becca's mixed a potion to dissolve Daemon's hooves and legs so he can have human ones and feet. He's a satyr, by the way. I just want to make certain what she's made won't hurt him."

"If it dissolves his legs and hooves, I'd say hurt is a given."

Heather wasn't certain she could watch his agony, but she had to stay close to protect him from Becca and also from himself. He shouldn't be doing this. "I was referring to permanently. Like, after his legs are gone, they won't grow back or they'll be even worse than they were, while feet sprout from his arms or somewhere else they shouldn't."

"What did she mix and how does it look?"

Heather read the ingredients in the primer and off the containers to Rowena. "The brew's an icky gray color with brown and green edges." She made a face. "The edges are moving."

"Bubbling?"

"No, slithering." She shivered.

"Sounds right. If anything bad happens, give me a call, I'll be here."

"Thanks. That's so sweet of you. I don't know how I'll ever repay—" High heels clicked against the hall floor. "She's coming back. Bye." Heather dropped the phone in her purse.

Becca stopped just inside the door, a large picnic basket hanging from her arm. She looked from Heather to Daemon and back. "What did you do?"

Time for the awful truth, since she couldn't lie. She went hot, cold, hot...

"She bitched at me for belching." Daemon let loose with an epic burp, truly loud and prolonged. Finished, he gave Heather a sly smile. "Sorry. Won't happen again." He stuffed three hash browns into his mouth.

Becca shook her head and pulled the newest ingredients from her basket—numerous bottles of booze and others that held pineapple, orange and lime juice. She filled a tall plastic glass with the various rums and brandy and splashed scant juices on top.

The booze odor nearly knocked Heather down. "Isn't that drink kind of strong?"

"If we're lucky, it'll have him flat on his ass."

Or kill him. "Daemon, you shouldn't be doing this."

A pancake hung from his mouth. Syrup ran down his chin. "Was this yours? Did you want it back?"

"No." She wrung her hands. "You shouldn't be going through with the treatment."

He eyed the potion, worry on his face. It dissipated quickly. "Whatever Becca mixed didn't dissolve the plastic, so I'm sure it'll be okay for me." He slapped his belly. "I've got a cast-iron stomach."

Heather bounced on her heels. "What if something goes wrong?"

"Hey." Becca frowned. "It won't. I matched the picture in the primer perfectly."

"I say let's do this." He shoved the pancake into his mouth and swallowed. "Wait."

Becca slouched against the counter. "Why?"

"I missed a cinnamon melt." He dispatched it quickly and slapped his hands against each other. "Okay, I'm ready...no matter what happens."

"You say that now but you might think differently later." Heather wished he'd like himself as much as she already did. "You're perfect just as you are. You could change your mind. You haven't even signed the contract yet."

"He hasn't?" Becca brought it to him along with a pen. "It's now or never. Heather, can you take care of his trash?"

As she cleaned up the empty wrappings and fretted, Daemon initialed every page, signed the last and gave her a soft smile. "It'll be all right."

Becca joined them, the zombie in one hand and her potion in the other.

Daemon reached for the booze.

She held it away from him. "Wait. I'm not sure which of these you should have first. That's not in the book."

Heather wanted to flee but couldn't abandon him. "Maybe he shouldn't have the zombie at all."

Daemon shot her a frown.

Becca regarded the two drinks. "If I mixed them together, that might be best."

"Or not." Heather clasped Becca's wrist to stop her. "What if mixing them together messes up the potion and it dissolves his arms or something else?"

He cupped his balls and cock protectively. "Let's be sure, all right?"

"Absolutely." Heather raced to her purse and pulled out her smartphone. "We should call Rowena and get her opinion so nothing's messed up."

Becca glared worse than Daemon had when Heather suggested he go without booze. "I followed the primer. The potion is right." She shouted, "Zoe! Get in here! Now!"

His head fell forward. "Aw, fuck."

The door flew open. Zoe's blouse hung over her plaid skirt, two buttons torn off. Smoke rose from her mussed hair. Her eyes flamed brightly. "Yo."

"Get ready to strap him in." Becca lifted the drinks. "Soon as I give him this."

"You got it."

Becca backed up to her primer and read. "The potion should start to work in less than two minutes." She spoke to Daemon. "How fast can you drink the zombie?"

"Three seconds tops. I haven't had one of those babies in months." He wiggled his fingers. "Give it to me."

"The potion first." She handed it over.

Zoe sniffed the concoction. "Smells great."

A backed-up sewer stunk less than it did. Heather swallowed repeatedly to keep from gagging.

Daemon pinched his nose and guzzled the mixture. He shuddered violently, swore and shoved the empty glass at Becca. With the zombie cupped in his hands, he drained the glass dry and smacked his lips approvingly.

No one budged.

Heather wasn't certain if anyone still breathed — it was that quiet.

A snarl from the next room broke the silence, along with a huge thud from something slamming against the wall.

Zoe looked over and shouted, "Don't let that bum get loose. I'll be there as soon as I can."

Daemon dropped the glass. It bounced on the floor. His eyes rolled up until only the whites showed.

Heather hurried to him. "Careful." She supported his head.

He dropped to the table, dead to the world.

Zoe was on him in a flash, redoing the restraints.

"Not so tight." Heather winced. "You'll hurt him."

"As if." Zoe pointed. "The potion's doing that."

A scream caught in Heather's throat. From his thighs down, there was nothing but bubbles and nasty hissing sounds like acid eating away flesh.

Zoe grinned.

Daemon moaned. His eyes flew open.

Heather flapped her hands. "Oh, no, he's awake."

"Maybe not." Zoe pinched the skin on his ribs.

He howled.

"Stop that, please." Heather yanked Zoe's hand away.

"We need more booze." Becca rushed to get it.

Daemon's agonized bellow filled the room. Becca poured rum and brandy down his throat. It didn't do any good. His complexion was beet red from his misery, eyes bulging. Sweat poured down his face.

"Don't. I'm begging you." Heather pulled Becca from him before she offered more liquor. "It's not working."

"Maybe there's another potion I can mix to put him out." She hurried to the primer.

Zoe inclined her head. "Right leg's gone."

Tears streamed from Daemon's eyes.

"Now the left one's going, going —"

"Quiet!" Alarmed at her behavior, Heather covered her mouth. "I shouldn't have been so rude. Forgive me, please?"

Zoe shrugged. "Sure."

With no other solution, Heather considered the only thing that might help a satyr forget his misery. Pure hard lust. She eased Daemon's hair from his damp face and brushed her lips over his.

"Hey." Zoe clamped Heather's shoulder.

She shook her off.

Daemon inhaled sharply. His mouth quivered against hers.

Her entire being opened even more to him. She snuggled her tongue between his lips and slipped it inside his hot, wet mouth.

Smoke from Zoe's hair and shoulders filled the room. "Stop that."

Heather eased closer to him. Daemon groaned and growled, the sounds pure male, his pain either gone or forgotten. He fought the restraints and tried to touch her. She rested her hand on his, doing for him what he couldn't do for her.

He sucked her tongue, inviting it inside.

She tasted sweet juice and rum on his lips, salt from the hash browns and his dazzling flavor, fresh as the outdoors, welcome as a caress.

Zoe grabbed Heather's arm.

She twisted free.

"No, don't." Becca pulled Zoe away. "Leave her alone. He's not in pain anymore."

Pleasure rolled off him in waves that crashed into Heather. She laced her fingers through his and held tight, her kiss gentle and comforting. Daemon sucked her tongue deeper into his mouth. She surrendered, giving her all, thrilled at his happy moans and indecent growls. Like the satyr he was, he took command and filled her mouth with his tongue. She enjoyed him with wonder and passion, her kiss sloppy and artless, totally satisfying.

Time lost all meaning. It seemed they'd always done this, there was no beginning, but there had to be an end. Needing a full breath, she eased her mouth from his and panted.

Daemon blew out a sigh and gazed at her lovingly.

She smiled.

His lids sank down and his head fell to the side.

Her stomach clenched. "Daemon?" She shook his shoulder.

"Relax." Becca tugged her away. "He just passed out."

Heather sagged against the nearest wall, limp from worry, spent from desire. She gulped air then couldn't breathe. His legs had returned, fully human, nicely muscular, the skin bronzed and roughened with short, dark hairs. Really nice, except for... "He hasn't got any feet!"

"I know." Becca rubbed her neck. "I forgot to ask what kind he wanted."

Heather hoped she wasn't serious. "Human. Like his legs. What else?"

Becca spoke through her teeth. "I know. But does he want the second toe longer than the first, shorter, what size should his feet be? It's all in the details."

Zoe checked his boot. "This is a thirteen."

"For his hooves." Heather gestured to the empty space beneath his ankles. "What about feet? Is he going to get any?"

Becca gestured dismissively. "Of course. I just need to figure out how they should look."

"We got vamps and that damn warlock in the other treatment rooms." Zoe jabbed her thumb in that direction. "Their feet should do as a prototype. Give me a sec and I'll twist off the warlock's and bring them in here for show and tell."

"Not a chance." Becca pointed at her. "No violence and I mean it. That's not what we do here."

Daemon not having feet came pretty close. Heather hated to nag Becca, but this had to be settled. "After you look at the vamps' or warlock's feet, while they're still attached, does that mean Daemon will suddenly grow a pair of his own?"

"I need to make a call." Becca tore from the room.

Heather prayed she was going to phone her mom and that Rowena could help. Unable to look at Daemon's incomplete form, she sweated and paced.

Zoe sat on the counter, swinging her legs.

Rarely had Heather been as irritated. "Shouldn't you be getting back to your warlock?"

"Not until the walls start shaking again or one falls in." Things were relatively quiet. "Besides, in here looks like more fun."

"How can you say that? This is Daemon's life."

"Doesn't mean it's not entertaining. A little advice as your friend — you need to chill. You worry too much."

She was right, of course, but Heather couldn't help it. Her thoughts grew even darker. Without feet, how would Daemon get around? He wouldn't be able to return to Couturie or boogie with mortal babes like he wanted. Her stomach twisted at him being with anyone else, but he wasn't looking for a good fairy who was too timid and nice to free her lust. He wanted someone smoking hot, like he was. Only now, he'd be a hunk without feet, a satyr without a home, doomed to stagger endlessly on his stumps and never have any fun.

She crossed the room repeatedly until she couldn't walk anymore. Slumped against the counter, she scoured the primer, hoping to find an answer. She paused on a spell that called for cremating frogs and wearing their ashes.

Becca rushed inside, smartphone in hand, a picture on the screen.

Heather craned her neck. "Is that someone's feet?"

"Eric's. He has nice toes." She mixed a new potion that smelled worse than the first, was black as oil and had the same consistency.

"Nice." Zoe's stomach growled.

Becca inclined her head toward Daemon. "Time to wake him, Heather. With a kiss if need be — don't let him see his legs."

As if she could be so cruel. She eased her hand beneath Daemon's head and ran her fingers down his bristly cheek.

His nostrils flared. His upper lip fluttered from a faint snore.

Her heart turned over in tenderness and longing. She kissed his temple, nose and gorgeous lips.

Daemon perked up. He sought her mouth, his passion demanding, insatiable and freaking nice. She held her hand out. Becca slapped the newest potion into her palm. Quick as could be, Heather pulled her mouth from Daemon's, pushed the glass to his lips and tilted it. "Drink."

He gagged and coughed.

"Swallow, please."

He did and shivered worse than he had earlier. "Fuck, that's shitty."

He wouldn't get an argument from her. She gave him the remaining brandy, half a bottle. He polished it off in seconds and conked out again.

Heather pecked his lips a final time, smoothed his hair back and held vigil.

His toes appeared first, looking exactly like Eric's, except these were suspended in space. Emptiness stretched between them and his bloody ankles.

Becca chewed her thumb, doubt and concern in her eyes.

Heather wanted to be sick.

His soles appeared next with other stuff filling in.

She liked the skeletal bones, tendons and guts, but wasn't certain he would if the potion stopped at this point. Even if he could hide the deformity with socks, wearing shoes or boots might hurt him. Unable to stand this any longer, she covered her eyes.

Zoe grunted. Or maybe she was stifling a laugh.

Heather couldn't take it. "Please don't say anything mean."

"I wasn't planning to. Hey. Look."

"Uh-uh. I can't."

"It's good. I swear."

His feet were intact and large, his toes long.

Becca checked them against the picture on the smartphone and wore a proud smile. "They're a perfect match for Eric's."

As far as Heather was concerned, Daemon's feet were even better looking than his. Not that she'd say such a heartless thing. "You did a good job."

"Thanks." Becca strutted to the table. "Now, for his tail and horns."

Breathy and guttural voices floated in and out of Daemon's consciousness. Someone rolled him onto his belly. Heather's powdery fragrance surrounded him. Zoe's sulfur odor chased the pleasant scent away.

He scrunched his nose. Smoke tickled it.

Zoe again, probably pissed.

She cleared her throat. "I got it."

He wondered what she had.

She pinched his tail at its base.

Daemon braced for pain. Didn't come. Remarkably, he was on his back once more and hadn't a clue how he got there. The wrist and ankle restraints held him fast. His tail didn't bunch beneath his ass any longer.

Someone stroked his hair gently. Heather?

Had to be. Her light touch felt better than great sex. However, the sour taste in his mouth ruined his arousal. He would've killed for some water. No, wait, another zombie. He tongued his parched lips and opened his eyes.

Heather leaned closer, relief and awe on her face.

Daemon felt the same. "Is the treatment over?"

"Uh-huh. Curl your toes."

He had some? Hot damn, that was great news. He was about to look but didn't. Couldn't. "I can't feel anything down there."

"Seriously?" Becca hurried to him.

Heather whimpered. "Do something."

Zoe jabbed her pen into his sole.

Sharp pain rocketed through him. He gasped.

"Not that." Heather smacked Zoe. "Oh, no, I'm so sorry. Forgive me."

"Fuck, fuck, fuck." He couldn't catch his breath. "That pissing hurt."

"Looks like he can feel stuff after all." Zoe arched one eyebrow. "It's a miracle."

Becca touched his shoulder. "Do your legs feel weak?"

"Not exactly." He panted. "More like weird. As if they're not really there." He strained to lift himself and wished he hadn't. Becca had done one helluva number on him. "Why'd you give me such ugly feet?"

She made a face.

Heather stroked his arm. "Curl your toes."

He tried but couldn't and finally confessed. "I don't know how."

"That's okay. I'll teach you."

"Do it fast." Zoe checked her watch and strode to the hall. "We'll need the room in fifteen."

Becca followed and stopped at the door. "You obviously have feeling in your feet, so they should be fine once you get used to them. We'll need you to come back for a few follow-up appointments just to make certain everything's cool. Heather can book you." Becca spoke to her. "Once you find out when he can come back, let Zoe know. She'll unstrap him and will escort him out. He can't stay here again."

Heather slumped.

Daemon felt bad for her. He waited until Becca's footfalls faded. "Think my belch turned her off?"

She fought a smile. "Let's get you comfortable." She undid his wrist restraints and worked on those around his ankles.

"Think your boss is gonna like that?"

"Becca's overly cautious because she doesn't know you."

"Neither do you. Not really."

"I'm not afraid." She regarded him with pure wonder, as she had yesterday before they'd kissed. "I trusted you even when you looked like a satyr, which I still say was perfectly all right."

The truth shone in her eyes and sounded in her sweet words.

Daemon was too moved to speak. No one had ever responded to him as Heather did.

She slipped her arm around his waist. "Try to stand and take your first steps. You can lean on me."

Who the fuck cared about walking? Her sweet nature and worry when he'd been crazy with pain did almost as much for Daemon's libido as if she'd taken his cock in her heated mouth. The promise of his rod sliding over her tongue and down her throat drove him wild, but he restrained himself and ran his knuckles over her cheek.

She turned into him. Color tinted her face. Desire flooded her eyes.

He hoped her newfound passion wasn't only because he finally had feet and toes. Could be she liked them more than she was willing to admit given her you-were-fine-with-your-hooves speech.

Daemon hopped off the table. His new legs felt as supple as concrete blocks and as weak as his old ones did when he'd drunk too much. Unsteady, he tottered.

She reached for him. "Careful."

He nodded even though taking care and being a good boy wasn't his plan. He hauled Heather up and sat her where he'd been.

Her blush deepened but she didn't scold.

He'd always love her for that. "Thanks."

"For what?"

"Worrying so much, easing my pain, giving me all your food, healing my bloody stumps, not taking the booze from me."

"I didn't mind. I don't. Except for the liquor."

He figured as much. "I don't want to talk about that." He cupped her beautiful face. "Most of all, thanks for this." He kissed her hard, deep, wet and long until he couldn't breathe. Gasping, he shoved her blouse up. Ribbons, flowers and lace decorated her super dainty bra. In white, of course.

He reeled.

She heaved air but arched her back, delivering herself to him rather than fighting what comes naturally.

Why, he didn't know unless she'd guzzled a few shots while he'd been out and they'd relaxed her. Whatever the reason, he pulled down her bra and exposed her cute little breasts. They trembled from her strained breathing. The nipples were a dusky rose, darker than he'd imagined and tight as could be. Had to be from him, not the temperature in here. If anything, the room was downright toasty.

Or possibly too hot. Her complexion got redder by the second. "Doing okay?"

A strangled sound tore from her. No words followed.

Daemon didn't want to pursue his questioning, but he didn't want to scare her either. She deserved a gentleman at all times. "Want me to keep going?"

Heather nodded so fiercely, her hair jumped over her shoulders onto his.

"Thanks. I swear this won't hurt." He licked her right areola and just about died at how sweet it tasted.

She swallowed hard and shivered.

If she told him to stop at this point, he wasn't certain he'd have the strength to pull back. He licked her again, cautiously so.

Gulping air, she wrapped her legs around his narrow hips.

If that wasn't an invitation to indulge in his base nature, he didn't know what was.

He lowered Heather to her back and sucked one breast while fondling the other. Her skin was softer than a new leaf, amazingly warm and perfumed with her natural scent. The beast in him awakened, wanting to be free. His balls and cock hurt like a sonofabitch. It took enormous will power to go slow and treat her gently.

She gripped his skull and pushed his head against her rather than away.

Damn, he'd really read her wrong. Never one to deny a lady what she wanted, he succumbed to his randy nature. As he feverishly sucked her nipple, he yanked her skirt up and caressed her velvety thigh.

She trembled in what could have been pleasure or renewed fear.

Hoping for delight, he touched her delicate panties, a confection boasting lace and bows. He bypassed the fluff, eased his fingers beneath the elastic edge and touched her cunt.

The room twirled. She wasn't only wet, she was dripping.

A growl rose in his throat. He shoved it down, stroked her cleft and paused on her clit. The small nub was nicely hard. He rubbed it.

Joyous wails burst from her. She dug her heels into his ass and pulled him closer.

He drove through her springy curls and thumbed her clit.

She moaned.

Footfalls pounded in the hall, racing here.

Zoe made a nasty noise. "I'll bet he's at it again."

She knew him too well.

Daemon should have stopped but couldn't. He tongued Heather's clit and plucked her nipples.

Becca, Constance and Zoe burst inside.

Zoe stomped on his feet, all ten toes.

Chapter Four

Heather perched on the needlepoint sofa in Becca's office, her fingers laced tightly, knees pressed together. She tensed for the worst.

Zoe paced and batted numerous ferns and other vegetation that got in her way. Constance blocked the door, her maroon turban and gown as somber as her face. Becca leaned against her antique desk and touched the topaz stones dangling from her navel. Their golden color matched her silk crop top and harem pants. The fabric and jewels shimmered in the warm glow pouring from her Tiffany lamp.

Cold with fear, Heather shrank against the cushion. "Are you going to fire me?"

Becca gaped. "Of course not."

"Let's cut to the chase." Constance crossed to Heather. "I'll lay my hands on your head and evaporate every last memory of that bad boy for you."

"No, please." She scooted away from her. "I don't want to forget Daemon. He's not a bad guy."

Zoe made a derisive noise. Smoke belched from her. Its horrible odor blocked the lovely plant scents.

"He's not." Heather wasn't one to argue, especially with good friends, but the time had come for her to take a stand. "I kissed him back."

Constance snickered. "Yeah, hon, we noticed."

Becca joined Heather on the sofa. "You're way out of your depth with him. He's been around."

"Hell, that man probably invented sex." Constance got a dreamy look. "His cock is so long it should have its own zip code. His balls, too."

Heat stung Heather's cheeks. "Constance, please."

"Sorry, sweetie, but Becca's right. If you've finally decided to date, you should start with someone closer to your strange worldview."

"Exactly." Becca's face tightened with worry. "There are plenty of ultraconservative-types who don't believe in booze, bad language, sex or fun of any kind."

"For themselves or the rest of us, amirite?" Constance exchanged a glance with Zoe and Becca. "They're literally the walking dead."

Or a good fairy's Prince Charming come true. Similar to the principled politicians Heather had read about. Unfortunately, one after the other got caught lying, cheating or stealing because none had been honorable at all. She'd about given up hope that any male was good, then Daemon had arrived. Trouble with a capital T. Sexy as sin, certainly lusty, but with what she sensed was a good core, filled with integrity unlike the others.

Becca patted Heather's hand. "Once you get the hang of things, you can work your way down from the saints to a moderate, maybe even a liberal."

Heather shook her head. No one would ever be like Daemon. He'd ruined her for other guys. "I have to think of Daemon now. His legs and feet are new because of what we did to him."

"Whoa, whoa, whoa." Zoe pointed. "What he wanted. We have his signed contract. If he's changed his mind about this, it's not our fault. Maybe I should talk to him."

"*No.*" Heather put out her hand terrified Zoe would leave him a bloody mess. "He hasn't complained about the treatment at all and I never said what Becca did to him was her fault."

"My fault?" She blinked. "You mean giving him great-looking feet?"

Zoe and Constance traded a glance.

Becca frowned. "What?"

Before everyone started arguing, Heather squeezed Becca's hand. "You did a wonderful job on Daemon. I'm not questioning that. But I do wonder about our after-service. We can't expect him to walk back to Couturie." She spoke to Zoe. "You practically broke his toes the way you stomped on them."

"It was the only way I could get him off you, considering how tightly you were holding on."

Not wanting to get into that, Heather returned to the real subject. "The forest is more than four miles from here. Way too far for him to walk on sore feet."

"Here's a thought." Zoe planted her hands on her hips. "Heal them first."

"They'd be sore again after he got there. It's a long walk."

"We're not disputing the distance." Becca looked at Zoe. "You could drive him there, right?"

"Only if I can hogtie him first and lash him to the roof."

"That won't solve anything," Heather gripped her knees. "We're all forgetting the most important thing. He doesn't have a tail, horns or hooves anymore. No one in the forest will recognize him. What if they jump Daemon and he gets hurt? And please don't say I can heal him if that happens. He'd have to come back here first. His misery would never end."

Becca slung her arm around Heather's shoulders. "I understand your concern. But, sweetie, we can't keep him here."

Constance plopped on the sofa arm. "We can't debate this forever, either. He has to go somewhere. Since I have a spare room at my place, I'll let him stay with me."

Heather shot to her feet. "Thank you, but no." She sensed what Constance would do once she got him alone. By tomorrow, she'd have his nude pictures plastered on her Facebook page. "I'm taking him home with me."

Constance screwed up her mouth.

Becca made a pained sound. "That's a bad idea."

"Will you fire me because of it?" Heather gestured to everyone. "Are you guys going to stop being my friends and the only family I have?"

"No."

They'd spoken as one. Even Zoe.

Becca stood and embraced Heather. "We're yours for life, sweetie. Nothing and no one will get rid of us."

She blinked back grateful tears.

"That doesn't mean we agree with what you're doing. It's foolish and you know it. If you're not careful, he's going to turn you inside out."

Constance smiled wantonly. "You lucky dog."

Becca elbowed her and spoke to Heather. "You have our numbers on speed dial. If he gives you any trouble, you call us. Understand?"

Heather nodded. If there was a problem, she would call. Of course, they hadn't defined exactly what that danger or difficulty was supposed to be.

Heather begged off her remaining shift to go home, a short walk from the office.

It proved a struggle for Daemon, even though she'd healed the damage Zoe had done to his poor toes. She'd tried to increase her power to strengthen his new body parts, but the magic he'd gone through had taken a greater toll on him than she would have guessed. Only time would help him get used to his feet and legs, which left him barely able to shuffle.

Heather kept her arm firmly around his waist and braced him.

He cupped her ass and squeezed.

Warmth rolled through her, his caress fueling her intense need for everything he was and could be — a guy who ate slowly, stifled his belches and behaved himself in public. Even with his daunting social habits, she still craved him. If she didn't set some boundaries soon, she'd lose her head like everyone said. "Daemon."

His fingers went slack.

"Thank you."

He didn't respond. He stared straight ahead.

A young woman wove through the tourists and trotted toward Heather and him. Dressed in a scarlet tank top, black running shorts and sneakers, she passed them then turned around and jogged backwards, her focus riveted on him, her smile downright predatory.

His steps slowed and stopped. He took the young woman in, undressing her with his eyes as he had Heather the night he'd shown up at the office.

Jealousy hit hard, hurting her belly and chest. She told herself it was stupid. She had no claim on him. Even so, she had to keep from ramming her heel into his toes as Zoe had. "If we don't get going, you'll never be able to take off your boots."

That got him moving. By the time they'd reached her front door, his face and hers were drenched in sweat from the trek and muggy weather. Thankfully, her building was only one story, no stairs to climb.

Daemon teetered into her living room. Breathing hard, he glanced from side-to-side, taking in the carpeting, walls, drapes, sofa and other furniture, everything in white. "Damn. This must be a real fucker to keep clean."

Heather shook her head. "Speaking of which, your language?"

He tottered to the pictures she'd hung on the wall. Most showed Becca, Zoe and Constance, except for her adoptive parents' photo. They sneered at the camera. Daemon regarded Zoe's pictures and made a face. "What about my language? You want me to talk Cajun or Creole now? I only know a little of both. I do pretty well with street slang, though. Hey, bro." He bobbed in place and bent his fingers into weird shapes as one would when having a fit. "You a gangsta or a wanksta? Confess to me, baby. It's cool." He leaned closer to her adopted parents' picture and grimaced. "You want me to keep talking like that?"

Heather was too tired to get into it. "No."

"These your folks?" He pointed.

"Uh-huh. I took that the last time they visited."

His eyebrows lifted. "Looks like they didn't have too good a time. What happened?"

During moments like these, she wished she could lie. Unable to, she lifted her shoulders.

"Did they give you a hard time?"

"You mean holler at me? No."

He tottered to her and cupped her chin. "What did they do? Tell me. You look really sad."

"I shouldn't." She forced a smile. "When I invited them here, I expected them to make themselves at home. It's not like it was a shock or anything that they did."

"Did they steal your stuff and you had to get new things?"

"No." Her laughter surprised her. "They ate everything I had. Even my lunch for work."

He curled his upper lip. "You should have called them on it."

She slumped. "Even if I'd wanted to, which I didn't, when I woke up, they were gone."

"Wow. That's cold. I'm sorry."

His empathy meant everything. She'd known so little in her life before she'd met her buddies at work. If she wasn't careful, she'd cry. "Thanks, I appreciate it. But I don't want you to get the wrong impression. They don't mean what they do. Someday things will be better between them and me." She hoped. Living through more heartache with the people who were supposed to care about her wasn't something she looked forward to. "We shouldn't be talking about them. You're what's important. Would you care for a bath?"

Surprise crossed his face. He sniffed himself. "Do I offend?"

"Absolutely not." She'd never known anyone who smelled so wonderful. "I thought you might like to soak, relax, enjoy yourself."

His lips curled up in an indecent smile.

She blushed hotly.

He calmed down and affected a puppy dog-look guys use to appease women. "A bath sounds nice. But I'll probably need help to get there. My legs and feet feel like raw fucking meat." He moaned pitifully.

Despite his language, Heather suppressed a smile at his terrible performance. "As to where you'll sleep... There's my sofa." It was half his length. "Or you could use the courtyard outside my kitchen. It's private and has a few trees, plus a bunch of plants. It'll keep you from getting homesick."

He chuckled. "I'm not."

"You might be. You can't go back now since you've changed. No one will recognize you."

He shrugged. "I'll handle it. Can I have a brew with my bath?"

"I don't have liquor here."

"Not to worry. I'll take care of it."

"How?"

He stopped fingering his ring. "I better ditch my boots before my feet swell too much." He leaned against her wall and tugged them off.

Heather pressed her hand to her chest. His toes resembled Vienna sausages, red and puffy, his feet the same. "Look what you've done to yourself."

"Hey, it wasn't my potion. Besides, Zoe pounding on my toes didn't help."

"She was wrong, but so were you for changing."

"Too late now."

Maybe not. He might be able to go back to what he was once he got the money for it.

Heather couldn't imagine how he'd managed to get any cash since he didn't have a job and lived in a forest. She wanted to ask but feared being too nosy. "Give me a sec and I'll heal your feet again."

He put out his hand to keep her from kneeling. "Later. The bath sounds better, if you don't mind."

She'd do anything, within reason, to make him feel better. "Lean on me." She slipped her arm around his waist. "I'll help you to the tub."

Daemon brushed his lips over her temple and pressed his bristly cheek to hers. "Thanks."

His breath was hot on her ear, his cock rigid as stone against her thigh. Trembling with arousal, she recalled Becca's admonition that he'd turn her inside out if she wasn't careful. She pulled her hand from his chest. "Sure."

In the bath, he blinked at the bright lights that made everything even whiter.

Heather sank next to the claw-foot tub and adjusted the water until it was comfortably warm. "I'll have this filled in no time." She looked over.

His hat, tee and jeans lay in a heap on the hallway carpet, leaving him spectacularly nude and fully human in appearance.

Her heart whapped against her chest.

He approached, his teeth gritted, features pained as they would be if he were walking on barbed wire.

Heather lifted her face. His shaft dangled inches from her mouth. The crown was as plump as a small fist, redder than a New Orleans's sunset, heat pouring from it, the scent male and musky.

Her pulse raced at the impossible and shameful desire coursing through her. Not that it changed anything. She wouldn't indulge in anything carnal. She couldn't.

She pressed her face against the hair on his groin, filled herself with his wondrous fragrance and quivered with need.

He groaned.

"This is so wrong." She rubbed her nose in his awesome curls.

"No, no. You're doing it right, just a little lower, babe." He clasped her head and guided her until his cock nestled against her mouth.

His flesh was hot and hard, his skin satiny.

Her lips trembled.

"Lower." He pushed gently.

Heather couldn't resist. She snaked her tongue down his shaft, traced the prominent veins and savored his faint saltiness.

He tasted better than a Quarter Pounder.

Hungry for more, she swirled her tongue over the head, delighted at the silky fluid that escaped the small slit. Never had she tasted anything as decadent or as wonderful. Needing it all, Heather slipped his meaty cock into her mouth.

Daemon bellowed enthusiastically and gripped her head, keeping her from pulling away.

Totally unnecessary. She was a good fairy, not nuts. She worked his plump balls gently and eased his cock from her mouth then slid it back inside until she'd taken about half in. Challenged and wanting, she opened her throat and slipped a few more inches inside. Wasn't easy, but she wanted to make him happy. Herself, too. Who would have thought something so wanton and wrong could feel so good?

His knees sagged, bumping into her. "More."

She didn't think that was possible.

"Please, babe. *Please.*"

No way could she resist or deny him. Doing her best, Heather slid his full length inside. Her nose rested on his musky curls.

He shuddered and swallowed loud. "No. It's still not enough."

That didn't make sense. She couldn't take his balls in her mouth too. No woman could.

Except maybe the babe who'd eyed him on the street.

New jealousy hit, giving her the courage to go for the gold. She pushed his sac toward her already-filled mouth and tried to stuff it inside.

Daemon gasped. "Holy shit, *stop.*" He staggered back and shifted his weight. "Ow, ow, ow."

She pushed up. "What's wrong?"

"My feet are fucking killing me."

"I didn't touch them."

"I know. You were hurting my boys." Breathing hard, he cradled his sac.

"You didn't want me to take them in my mouth?"

"Sure, once my cock was out of it."

Feeling like a fool, she nodded and walked on her knees to him. "I'll do your, uh, boys now."

"Get undressed first."

She pressed her hands to her high collar and leaned away from him.

"Please?" He pushed out his bottom lip. "It'll be more fun if we can do each other at the same time. You know, lick, suck and blast off?"

That sounded totally depraved but oddly fair, except for the logistics. "I'm not sure what you mean."

"Ditch your duds and I'll show you."

"What about your bath?"

"It can wait." He wobbled to the tub and tried to twist the faucet. When nothing happened, he swore and twisted harder.

"If you want the water off, you turn the knobs on either side."

"On it." After wrenching them in the wrong direction, he got it right and killed the flow.

Steam rose from the tub and crowded the bathroom, making everything hazy, warm and surreal.

He stepped closer, clenched his jaw and panted. "Want me to help you undress?"

If he didn't, she might never move from this spot. She nodded.

Faster than Heather had ever undressed herself, Daemon had her stripped bare. She covered her breasts with one hand, her curls with the other.

He ran his knuckles across her cheek as he had in the treatment room. Such a tender, gentle gesture. She kissed his palm.

Daemon curled his fingers. "Lie down. No, wait. Fix my feet first, please."

Once she'd healed him, he pointed at her. "Don't move." He grabbed his tee and jeans, rolled them into a makeshift pillow and placed them on the tile. "Go on. I'll help you."

The second she was on the floor, he lifted her arms and spread her legs. "Let me just look at you...all of you."

Heat pulsed through her. She broke out in a cold sweat.

Enchantment filled his amazing eyes. "God, you're like starshine. I've never seen anyone so beautiful."

She laughed self-consciously. "I'm really flat." The girl on the street had been bustier than Becca, which he seemed to like. "Don't you think?"

"Hell, no." He grinned. "You're just right. Let's get down to business." He faced away, straddled her and stretched out.

His balls and rod dangled like succulent fruit above her lips. Before Heather knew what to think about that, Daemon had already pulled up her legs and fastened his mouth on her uh…her…uh…

Pussy.

What a naughty yet glorious word. No wonder the clients used it when they tried to seduce the staff. She squirmed closer.

Daemon tongued her cleft, pulled at her curls with his teeth and licked her clit.

Shock, pleasure, alarm and outrageous desire raged through her. *Wow.* She'd never known such decadent yet exquisite feelings existed. She'd wasted too much time being good. That wasn't going to happen again. Surrendering to passion, she cupped Daemon's balls and lapped his wrinkly, hair-roughened skin.

His tongue paused on her nub. He panted hard then dove back in, holding her clit between his teeth, licking it relentlessly, driving her wild.

Heat whisked up Heather's arms and down her legs. Dizzy with lust, she went for broke and eased his right ball into her mouth.

Daemon howled but didn't pull away.

Reassured he liked what she did, she sucked and licked then tightened her hold on his rigid shaft and stroked it vigorously.

He squirmed, gasped around her nub and finally curled his toes.

Something he hadn't known how to do before, but did now because of her.

Tears blurred her vision. Affection for him flooded Heather and reached her soul. Finished with his right ball, she tended to his left.

He sucked her clit.

Her pussy ached dully, feeling heavy and congested, needy of his mouth and tongue. The room spun, the air so thick she could scarcely breathe. Trembling with anticipation and unspent pleasure, she released his ball, slipped his rod into her mouth and guided his full length inside.

He made sounds that proved the delight they delivered to each other — bliss more powerful than all the money in the world, as sacred as true friendship and love and having a family to come home to, people who cared.

She'd cherish this moment forever.

As he worked her sex, she ran her tongue down his thick rod and discovered his pleasure spot, the bumpy skin on his crown. She licked it mercilessly, as he did her nub.

They squirmed and panted, driving each other closer to the brink.

Heather was perilously near.

Daemon stroked the furrow between her cheeks and touched her anus.

She shattered. Warmth and pure delight dashed through her. It felt like soaring above the Earth then tumbling through clouds and finally landing on a soft, grassy field scented with wildflowers. Surrounded by comfort and embraced by ecstasy she'd never known.

She tried to stop gasping so she could tend to Daemon, loving him as he had her. Calmed somewhat, she licked his shaft lazily.

He squirmed and made noises that sounded more animal than human.

Guessing he couldn't take much more, she cradled his balls.

He went rigid, blasted off as he'd predicted and shuddered.

His rich creamy cum spurted into her mouth.

Surprised, she froze.

"Fuck, fuck, fuck. I shouldn't have done that. Sorry." He grabbed his rod.

Heather pushed his hand away, not willing to let him go. Uncertain what to expect, she tongued his offering. It tasted like him, life and beginning love.

Pleasure flooded her.

Totally beat, Daemon reclined in the tub on the left side, his head against the tall lip, his foot in Heather's small hands. Water lapped her precious boobs and sweet nipples. He'd propped her right foot on his left shoulder and her left on the other, spreading her wide.

Given her intense blush, her eyes seemed even greener.

Somehow, Daemon found her reaction beguiling and figured his grin was feral as hell, filled with reckless hunger. The way he'd been as a youngster when everything had been so new. Who would have guessed he'd get tired of it?

Would he be the same with Heather?

The thought came from nowhere. His stomach churned.

She stopped massaging his toes. "Are you in pain?"

Not physically, but emotionally and more than Daemon cared to admit. He'd gone through that god-awful treatment so he could have a good time with mortal women, not hole up here with a semi-virtuous fairy.

He should leave before he corrupted her further.

"Daemon?"

Unable to move or breathe, he did neither until his lungs burned. He gasped at the discomfort and gulped air.

She pushed up. Her feet fell in the tub and splashed water on him. "Are you all right?"

"No." He wiped drops from his face. "You moved."

He propped her legs on either side of the tub. The swishing water didn't hide her cunt. It was more beautiful than he recalled, her bush as light as the hair on her head, her folds wonderfully rosy and fragile-looking. Something inside him shifted again, part pleasure, part fear, neither emotion understandable.

She pulled in her shoulders, embarrassment in her eyes. "This isn't comfortable."

"Sorry." He planted her soles on his pecs. "Better?"

Her blush went from bright red to deep scarlet. "This is really wrong."

He vaguely recalled her saying something similar earlier. She'd been loving his balls and cock at the time. Whatever he'd said in response hadn't killed her passion. Now was different. Unless he got up and slipped his rod or nuts back into her mouth, he and she were probably going to have to talk. He braced himself for the worst. "Define wrong."

Reluctance flashed across her face followed by resolve.

She was going to tell him the score no matter how much her words might hurt or disappoint. He slumped. "Go on. I'm listening."

He had no other choice.

She pulled in a huge breath. "We're naked. We sucked each other's…" She shook her head.

"Want me to help you with the terms? I know every one. There's —"

"That's okay. I've heard them all."

He doubted that. "They're just words, you know."

Her blush deepened. "Not in my world."

If he lived there, he'd die. She probably would, too, after experiencing life as it should be. "Did you enjoy yourself while we were messing around?" He stroked her inner thigh.

Her nostrils flared slightly. She got a contented, faraway look on her face. "I-I-I…"

"You what?"

"Forgot what you asked."

"Doesn't matter. Just relax." He spoke as softly as he could. "Once we finish soaking, we'll get something to eat and go to bed. Hell, why don't we just eat in bed?"

She pulled her feet off him. One heel fell on his hip, the other on his rod and boys.

Searing pain tore through him. "*Jeez-us.*"

"Oh, no, I'm so sorry. Let me make it better." While struggling to get up, she kicked his thigh and rammed her shoulder against his knee but eventually grabbed his cock and stroked him like she meant it. "Feel good?"

Way better than his other bruised body parts. "Uh-huh." He got super hard, amazingly fast, precisely as he had when he was younger.

She noticed his arousal, dropped his shaft like it scalded her and scooted back.

Daemon couldn't keep up with her. Hot one minute. Cold the next. Downright frozen now. She'd pulled her knees to her chest, hiding herself. Maybe they did need to talk. "No matter what you've been taught or think, sex isn't bad. Without it, Earth would be a ghost town, if you get my drift."

She gave him a surprisingly pissy look for a good fairy. "I'm innocent, not dumb. I know sex is a necessary part of life, but you're supposed to save it for someone special."

He must have missed the memo. Wanting to lighten the moment, he slumped. "I'm not special to you?"

Heather looked stricken but recovered quickly.

He figured she was onto his teasing.

She leaned toward him. "How important am I to you?"

"Very." He'd answered without thinking, meaning what he said. She'd stood by him at that madhouse where she worked. She'd bought him breakfast without him having to beg. She'd eased his pain, let him have the booze and kept telling him he was fine as a satyr. He didn't need to change, except for his language, eating habits and belching. Even with that, she'd accepted him. Warts and all.

Of course, getting her to trust him completely was another matter.

Heather searched his face as a female does when she's not certain whether to believe a guy or not.

Stumped on how to convince her, he had no other choice except to be direct. "Want me to leave?"

She chewed her lip but shook her head.

"What me to get dressed?"

Her attention fell to his pecs and lower. Her hungry-dreamy gaze returned. "I'm a virgin."

"I figured as much. And it's no biggie — we all start out like that."

She sagged. "You don't understand. This goes against my beliefs."

"Soaking in a tub?"

"Being naked with you. Sucking you. Enjoying you."

"Maybe your beliefs are wrong or mistaken."

She tried to frown, even gritting her teeth from the effort.

He held up his hands in surrender. "I'm just sayin'."

"I don't know what to do."

"That's cool. But what do you want? Deep down where the sun don't shine?"

She ground her fist into her forehead, sighed repeatedly then fell into his arms.

Water surged over the tub.

They kissed themselves dizzy.

He came up first for air. "Let's take this to the floor where we'll have more room."

He'd never sounded as husky. His deep rasp softened Heather's bones.

When she didn't say no or yes to his suggestion, since she was too busy sucking his throat, Daemon cupped her butt, spread her cheeks and explored her intimate parts.

Riotous pleasure whipped through her.

This had to stop. Not only had she given him a humongous hickey, they were practically welded together. She wiggled away. "You need a shave."

Before he could stop her, she left the tub and returned, her Venus disposable razor in one hand, her sweetly scented shaving cream in the other.

He regarded both items skeptically. "I may have lived in a forest, but I know what pink means. It's for girls."

"Not always."

"Then you're saying guys use that stuff, too?" He gestured to her equipment.

If only she could lie. "Not as a rule. But I bet they wish they could if they weren't so concerned about their masculinity." She stroked his neck. "That's not something you'll ever have to worry about."

"Yeah?" His goofy smile made her day. "Have at it then."

Once she'd covered his face and neck with rich pink foam, he scraped a fingerful off, smeared it on her nipples and snaked out his tongue.

"No." She danced away. "You can't eat it."

"Why? Can't taste any worse than the potions."

He had a point. "Let me shave you." If she didn't do something nonsexual, there'd be no telling where tonight might end.

Standing behind him, Heather eased his head up, leaned over to see what she was doing and put her razor on his throat.

He licked her breast.

His tongue's wet heat tore through her ruthlessly. She jerked her hand.

He yelped.

"Sorry." She healed the cut. "Don't move or I might nick you again."

"I'll take my chances."

Did he ever. By the time she'd hacked off his stubble, her boobs and nipples were damp from his mouth, her skin flushed from unspeakable arousal. She'd cut him so many times, she stopped counting.

Apart from an occasional muttered oath, Daemon never complained.

And Zoe thought he wasn't a good guy.

"Let me help you up." Heather offered her arm.

"Are we leaving this room?"

"Yeah. But I have to towel you off first or you'll leave puddles."

"Is that bad?"

"I'd have to dry out the carpet and wax the floors again."

Confusion sparked in his eyes. "Okay. I never realized how simple things were in Couturie. There, the sun dried me after a swim."

"Do you want to go to my courtyard? There's a chair out there."

"Naw. I'll shake the moisture off like a dog or cat does. Squirrels do it, too. That works great."

Until a mortal saw him doing it. "All that movement could hurt your feet. Let me get you dry. I'll be gentle."

She patted his legs with great care and spent too much time on his balls and cock.

He made a contented sound. "That feels amazing. Way better than the sun. Don't stop."

No matter how hard Heather tried, she couldn't. His lovely rod swelled appreciatively from her dedicated attention. His sac hugged his body, ready for more play.

He gave her a warm and sexy smile filled with tenderness and arousal.

She wanted to take him to her bedroom but resisted the smutty thought and tossed the towel on the sink. "It's not good for you to be standing so long. Sit on the toilet and I'll help you with your jeans."

"Do I have to wear them? They scrape my legs. My skin is still kind of raw from the potion."

Heather dropped his clothes. "No. You're fine as you are." She couldn't imagine any guy being better. "Once we're in the living room, we can watch TV while we have dinner. What do you like to eat?"

He scratched his underarm. "Food."

"What kind?"

"Meat and stuff." His face brightened. "Do you have McDonald's breakfast menu here?"

"Sorry, no. If you want that, I'd have to get dressed and walk to the restaurant." And leave him here. She was afraid to consider what mischief he might get into. Worse, if her neighbors saw him and they had a conversation... "I could order a pizza. Have you ever had one?"

"Try several. A few years back, mortals were having a party in the forest. This guy showed up with fifteen of those babies. Before he got them to his friends, a buddy of mine shoved him and snatched the pies. I ate eight by myself." He laughed. "I could've gone up to ten, but I didn't want to be a pig. Pizza's great."

Thankfully, she'd gotten paid yesterday. After helping him to the sofa, she ordered ten large pizzas with the works for him and a small cheese one for herself. With dinner settled, she remembered her nudity. "I better get dressed."

He didn't seem surprised by her comment, only dismayed.

Before he got too bummed, she had to set him straight. "I'm not getting dressed because I'm shy, which I am. Or because I don't like you looking at me. I do, within reason, of course. However, when the pizza guy gets here, I have to open the door. You don't want him to see me like this, do you?"

"Hell, no."

His possessiveness thrilled her. "Me, neither. You need to cover yourself, too."

"Okay." He dropped the throw pillows on his feet.

"No. You need to cover your…uh…your…"

"What? My face? Head? Shoulders? Chest—"

"Lower."

"My stomach?"

"Down more."

Understanding lit his face. "Ah, my cock." His ginormous erection pointed at her cleft. Daemon's chest puffed out. "Is his shaft a lot smaller than mine? Will I make him feel bad if he sees what I have?"

"No. I mean, not exactly. You have to cover stuff on yourself that might offend people."

He frowned. "I did. My feet are the ugliest thing on me."

She wasn't certain if he was yanking her chain or not. "No part of you is ugly. Cover your groin. It's what civilized people do even in their own homes."

"That's stupid."

"You should have thought of that before you went through the change."

He said no more on the matter.

Once the pizza came, he chomped happily on the food. "What are we going to watch? Do you have *Avatar* here?"

"No. I have basic cable, no extras like movie channels. There's a *Dancing with the Stars* marathon on tonight."

"Will it cut out before it's over?"

"Not that I know of."

He beamed. "Great. Let's watch it."

They did, him nude and unashamed, her clothed, uptight and longing.

Heather hated to doubt him but each time a beautiful film or TV star competed, she worried about his arousal. No matter how built or sexy the babes were, he remained flaccid. She'd never known a guy's equipment could be better than a lie detector.

"Whoa." He swallowed the pizza in his mouth and pointed the remaining wedge at the screen. "See that girl in the red sparkly thing?"

His cock still hadn't inflated. "What about her?"

"Can you order what she's wearing like you did the pizza? That'd look great on you."

His sweet comment touched her. Dismay followed. "Don't you like me in white?"

He stopped chomping on his food. "As long as you do, yeah. I just thought… Forget what I was thinking. As far as I'm concerned, nothing can match your nudity."

On that happy note, he hunkered down for the other episodes.

Somewhere during the sixth one, she drifted into a dreamless sleep and woke near dawn, her head pillowed by his flaccid cock and sac. He smelled awesome, rich and musky, way better than the dark green bushes surrounding her TV. The vegetation hadn't been there last night.

She bolted upright.

Empty Coors cans littered her cocktail table.

Daemon released another snore. His arms were outstretched on the sofa, his head resting against a cushion, his mouth hanging open.

Heather resisted the urge to kiss him or press her face to his chest hair and fill herself with his scent. "What happened?"

No answer.

She shook his shoulder.

His eyelids parted.

"Why are there plants in here?" She gestured to them. "Where'd the beer come from?"

Daemon stopped smacking his lips and looked guilty. "It's complicated."

He offered nothing else.

Chapter Five

Heather arrived fifteen minutes early to work, the same as always.

Constance hurried down the hall and called out to the others. "She's here."

Zoe rushed from a treatment room, Becca close on her heels. They stared at Heather's makeup-free face, her hair worn parted in the middle, no different from times past, her blouse, jeans and sandals, all in white, the color fashionable until after Labor Day. Then she'd have to switch to off-white.

She might as well have worn ecru or the red sparkly gown Daemon liked given their disapproving looks. As one, they stepped closer.

Heather edged back.

They followed.

She hurried behind her chair, bumped into a plant and stopped. "What?"

Constance shook her turbaned head. Today, her headdress and gown were lime green slashed with pink. "The Eagle has not landed."

Becca and Zoe nodded. Relief flooded their faces.

"Good morning." Becca offered a pleasant smile.

Zoe bared her teeth. "Yeah, good morning."

Heather gripped her chair. "Hi. Have a good day. Please."

They exchanged a glance with each other and Constance. Huddled close, they trooped down the hall whispering furiously to each other.

Heather sank to her chair. She wanted to ask what Constance meant by her eagle comment but googled the phrase instead. More than fifty-nine million hits came up but only for the eagle has landed, which had several meanings. It was an old movie about Germans and Hitler, what an astronaut had said when he landed on the moon and slang for teachers getting their paychecks.

None made sense unless Constance meant there'd be no pay for Heather next week because another client had stiffed them and they were going to keep her wages to make up for it.

Didn't seem fair, but at least she wouldn't have to hassle with transferring funds from her account as she usually did.

She read further and stilled. According to the Urban Dictionary, the phrase meant two people had finally slept together.

Heather buried her face in her hands, her cheeks burning. They'd guessed what had happened, or rather hadn't happened, last night with Daemon.

The memories returned in full living color, along with how he'd dodged her questions about the bushes and booze.

Heather ground her fists into her eyes, wishing she'd had the nerve to press him on that and to have crawled all over him, begging him to fill her. Although she had ached for physical intimacy this morning, she'd hurried into the shower instead. Despite his still-aching feet, Daemon had joined her. He'd washed her back carefully, her boobs and mound lustily, sucked her nipples and licked her clit until she came twice. Losing control, she'd given him some serious head, made breakfast and reminded him not to go outside nude, speak to any neighbor, or anyone else for that matter, and to be on time for today's appointment.

He'd nodded and devoured his fifteen Eggos drenched in syrup and butter, enjoying them as he did everything in life. Recklessly. Freely. Decadently.

As she would have liked.

Heather gripped her chair. Even if celibacy made her nuts, she couldn't succumb to his charms.

She tried to control her frustration, but it mounted, everything she hadn't noticed before bugging her now. Especially the howls, hisses and wails. Nails clawing a blackboard would have been less annoying. Unglued, she rammed her pencil into the electric sharpener. The dumb device fell to the floor.

A were traipsed to her desk. "Hey. I need to book an appointment, same time next week."

She growled. "Give me a minute, all right? I. Am. Busy." She flung the sharpener against the wall.

He stepped back. "Sure. Take your time."

"Wait, I'm sorry."

"Okay."

"No, it's not." She rammed her fist into her desk. "I don't know what to do."

"I'll call later to make an appointment." He fled.

Heather wanted to bolt, too, but couldn't leave her stupid desk. She brought up the late accounts and saw red, remembering her last encounter with Satan. How he'd dismissed her and she'd been too willing to cover his payments with her hard-earned money.

She'd forgotten about that because of Daemon and was glad she had. She needed to scream at someone now and figured it might as well be the Prince of Darkness.

After a five-minute wait, his image filled her screen. Today, he was grandfatherly. White hair dangled over his forehead and touched his shaggy eyebrows. An equally white mustache drooped over his gentle smile. Black-rimmed eyeglasses, sagging jowls and a paunchy figure made him seem extra cuddly and harmless.

Knowing better, Heather got straight to the point. "You owe us money, mister. If you don't like what your grandson did, take it up with him, but we expect to be paid. We can and will affect your credit rating."

His light blue eyes turned to cobalt then charcoal. Flames raged within them.

Too frustrated to be frightened, Heather leaned toward the screen. "You have twenty-four hours before we turn you over to our collectors. Trust me, you don't want zombies down there, hounding you for eternity. No matter what *The Walking Dead* claims, even a bullet through their heads and decapitation doesn't stop them. Nothing does. Not even you."

Smoke poured from him as it always did with Zoe. "Watch it, sister. I can make your life hell."

"As if it isn't already? I don't know what to do. I want to sob, scream, run!"

Confusion raced across his features. He frowned. "PMS?"

Heather snarled. "I wish."

"Take it easy."

"I can't. I'm—"

Daemon shuffled inside.

"Sorry, gotta go." She turned off the webcam and raced to Daemon.

Pain contorted his sweaty face.

Heather slipped her arm around his waist, alarmed at how he shivered. "Your feet still hurt that bad?"

"Not as much as my fucking head. I've got a bitchin' hangover. It hit right after I drank all the syrup. Damn sugar."

More like the stupid booze he'd had last night. She smacked his hard belly.

Daemon leaned down to her. "Don't be mad. Help me please."

He was killing her. Worse, he was important to Heather. Too important. She should have listened to Becca but couldn't turn time back now. Wanting to ease his pain, she eased her fingers through his thick locks and massaged his scalp.

He sighed loudly.

Constance zipped from her office and joined them. "I thought I heard you two. Remember, if he needs his memories removed, only I can help."

"Thanks, but, no. He has a headache." Heather stroked his skull. "Better?"

"Shit, yeah. Now only my feet hurt."

Constance regarded them. "Zoe jumped on you again?"

"No. Excuse us." Heather helped him to a table in the nearest treatment room, closed the door on Constance and spoke through the barrier. "We'll be fine."

Constance sniffed. "Uh-huh."

Sunlight poured through the open shutters, caressing Daemon. The bright rays turned his bronze skin to gold and lightened his tea-colored eyes and dark hair.

Heather's heart stuttered at his male beauty and heavenly smile, so welcoming and sweet with a whole lot of sin beneath it.

Hardly the kind of guy a good fairy should end up with, but who was she to argue with Fate and what she'd always needed but hadn't realized until now? Adhering to the straight and narrow could never match being with him.

She jumped in his arms, slipped hers around his shoulders and wrapped her legs about his hips.

He stumbled back.

She'd forgotten his poor feet. "I'm so sorry. This must be hurting you. I'll get down."

"Like hell." He cupped her ass and claimed her mouth.

They kissed as if Satan were ready to separate them for eternity, the noises they made almost as loud as the shrieks and groans thundering from the other rooms. Heather tugged Daemon's tee, needing him closer. He pumped his groin into her pussy, telling Heather what they both wanted the most.

It was inevitable unless she fought her wayward urges.

Never had she felt as weary, not even when she'd been on her own without money or skills. Then, Becca had found her and made certain she was all right.

Now, Daemon would do the same. He'd show her the ways of the flesh and would take care with her heart. It's what she had to believe. That good guys were out there and he was the absolute best. Without hope and trust, what was left?

The door opened.

Becca's witchy perfume scented the area. Her foot tapped, tapped, tapped.

Heather knew what was coming but she still went at Daemon, practically devouring him. He did the same with her.

More foot tapping. "Ah, guys?"

It seemed silly to stop, so she enjoyed him one last time before pulling her mouth free. Back on her feet, she smoothed her blouse and jeans. "I'm worried. His feet still hurt."

Constance leaned against the jamb. "Putting your tongue down his throat certainly won't help."

Becca elbowed her. "Heather, sweetie, your extra weight isn't doing him any good."

"I don't mind." Daemon draped his arm over Heather's shoulders, grabbed her boob and pulled her close.

Her cheeks stung. She pulled away and shook her head.

Daemon looked lost. "What?"

"Remember what I said about civilized people?"

"Hell, yeah. My cock's covered."

Constance turned away. Her shoulders shook with quiet laughter.

Heather would have preferred another round with Satan to this. With her dignity in shreds, she spoke to Becca. "Should his feet still hurt? I keep healing them but it doesn't last. I tried to strengthen his legs but my power had no effect. Did you give him the same potion the sea witch gave the little mermaid to make her miserable?"

"Wait." Daemon held up his hand. "Are you talking about the cautionary tale?"

Heather nodded.

"I didn't give him anything like that." Becca's face said he and Heather were lunatics. "That's a story. This is for real. Let's take a look at your feet."

They were still swollen, though not as much as yesterday and weren't as red.

Becca straightened. "Soak them when you get back to Heather's. Don't overdo the walking. They should be fine."

He splayed his toes. "Will they stop looking so ugly?"

She bristled. "They're beautiful. Exactly like Eric's."

Constance leaned toward Heather. "Proof love is blind."

Heat rushed through her. Since she thought Daemon's feet were better looking than Eric's that had to mean she'd already fallen even harder than she'd imagined. She lifted her face to his.

Daemon's mild manner grew alarmed. "What?"

"Leave the romance for your place." Becca pointed at them. "This is a business, not a hotel."

Once Becca and Constance left, Heather clasped Daemon's hand. "Tonight."

"What about it?"

"You teach me everything I need to know about…about…"

"Sex?"

She nodded.

His eyes rounded. "You're sure?"

No, but her heart wouldn't allow another delay. Unable to lie, she spoke the truth, "Tonight. As soon as I get back from work."

Her day dragged in a way it hadn't before. The wails, hisses and growls not only annoyed Heather—each new one made her flinch. Unable to concentrate on anything, she booked a were and a hyena shifter at the same time. Zoe had to pull them apart before they destroyed each other and the room.

Heather forgot to order blood for the vamps and make follow-up calls to clients who had outstanding appointments. The few walk-ins had to keep repeating themselves as she worked on their intake forms, her thoughts drifting too much for her to retain anything they'd said.

When she had a moment alone, she wrote a list for what she'd need tonight. Food certainly, since Daemon liked to eat. Nothing sweet, though, so he wouldn't get a hangover. No booze, either. She couldn't bring herself to buy it nor figure out where he'd gotten the Coors or bushes, for that matter. She didn't bother to ponder birth control. Fairies were fertile only once a year, at Christmas. Such a sweet, festive time. No way could tonight alter that, no matter how hot Daemon was.

This was actually going to happen. She thrummed in expectation and shivered in doubt.

At last, the time came to take off. She stopped at the front door. "Good night, everyone. Hope you have a wonderful evening."

Before anyone could return her farewell, she fled the office.

She returned to her apartment with steak, prime rib, deli meats, cheese in numerous varieties, potato salad, coleslaw, pizza and junk food. Holding the bags in one arm, she unlocked her door and pushed it open but didn't step inside.

Crimson panels hung on her living room walls, gold silk tassels dangling between them. Incense burned in bronze bowls placed on low tables, the wood dark and old, possibly antique. Deep-red candles filled the space. Their flickering flames ate away the shadows and lent a hedonistic feel to the room and the huge four-poster bed that stood where her sofa and TV had once been. Sensuous music with an ancient beat pumped from everywhere, even though she hadn't heard it outside. The deafening bass kept time with her sprinting pulse.

Heather dropped her bags. They hit the scarlet carpeting, which used to be white.

Naked, Daemon limped into the room, flashed a smile and spied something on a table. His grin faded. He crumpled the papers and pushed the wad beneath the mattress adorned in purple silk sheets and pillows.

"What did you just hide?" Heather closed the door and locked it before the apartment manager saw what Daemon had done to this place. "What is all this?"

He rocked on his heels. "What women want."

She hoped he didn't mean a brothel. "How'd you get this stuff in here?"

He rubbed his neck. "I have connections. What's in the bags?"

"Food."

"Awesome." He gave her a deep, lingering kiss with lots of tongue.

She slumped against him.

Daemon moaned. He grabbed her bags and carried them to the kitchen.

Still panting from her arousal, Heather prayed he hadn't stolen this stuff from a stranger with horrible taste. If he had, the cops would show up and haul him to jail. "Did you pay for these things?"

He put away the groceries. "More than you can imagine."

She had no idea what he meant. "The meat goes in the fridge, not the dishwasher."

"On it." He turned a slow circle, his gaze sweeping.

She guessed he was trying to determine what item was the fridge. "Tall white thing to the left. It's making a humming sound."

He nodded.

"Does this stuff belong to you?" She gestured to the bed. "Or someone else?"

He tossed the Cool Ranch Doritos in the freezer and joined her. "It's ours for as long as we want." He cupped her breasts and flicked his thumbs over the nipples.

Her legs went rubbery. She fought for air.

"Did I pick the wrong colors?" He looked stricken. "Have you changed your mind?"

What was the matter with her? He'd gone to enormous trouble and her only concern was whether he'd stolen the tacky furnishings. Shamed by her doubt, Heather melted into him and pressed her mouth to his throat, the hickey she'd left yesterday. "No, I haven't changed my mind."

"You like what I've done?"

She nodded. It wasn't a lie. She liked that he'd cared enough to please her. "What you did is wonderful."

His bear hug squeezed her breathless. He carried her to the bed and placed her gently on the cool, slippery sheets. "I thought I'd die today waiting for this."

"Me, too."

His gaze softened. "There's no reason to be afraid."

Heather wasn't any longer. Hope and wonder filled her. She opened her arms to him.

Daemon licked her thumb. "Do you like when I do that? I saw a movie once where the actor did the same with his lady. It proved he was a gentleman. I won't do it if you don't like it."

"I love it."

He smiled. "I thought you would, since you're more of a lady than that actress will ever be. Let's get you out of these nasty clothes."

She laughed. "Does wearing clothes bother you?"

He tossed her sandals over his shoulder and pulled down her panties and jeans at the same time. "Sure. If they interfere with this."

His lips brushed her delicate curls.

Heather's breath caught.

After he dropped her garments on the floor, Daemon leaned over her. His hair swung forward and grazed his bristly jaw. He unbuttoned her blouse and shoved the ends apart.

Her nipples constricted from his ardent attention.

He touched the tiny bows and rosebuds on her bra and undid the front clasp to bare her breasts.

Moisture seeped from her pussy. She couldn't have been wetter for him.

His cock brushed her leg, leaving pre-cum in its wake, his arousal undeniable. In the candlelight, he was more than magnificent. He resembled pirates from romance novels, his long hair shiny and clean, skin burnished and scented with his wonderful masculine fragrance.

He pitched her remaining garments aside and looked at her.

Heather wanted to hide her small breasts. She fought the urge, needing to give him her all. She breathed as slowly as she could and let him look his fill.

His broad grin said he liked what she'd done. He touched her slit.

She gasped in satisfaction.

He released his own pleasured moan. "I won't hurt you."

"I know." She gripped his hair and brought his mouth to hers.

His kiss was tender and searching, his lips molding to hers to say they'd always belonged together. Nothing else would do.

Heather matched his pace, her tongue playing with his. She felt his smile and grinned in return.

On a pleased grunt, he deepened their kiss and plunged his tongue inside her mouth, tasting her as she sucked him.

His scent, touch, weight and warmth comforted and thrilled. Unable to touch him enough, she stroked his shoulders, back and the furrow between his cheeks.

His uncivilized growl filled the room. He ground his cock against her thigh.

Loving that and their slow, lazy kiss, she sucked his tongue deeper and stroked his balls lightly.

He groaned against her mouth. The vibration made her lips tingle.

Kissing him harder, she caressed his cock. Moisture seeped from the crown. She stroked it over the spot she liked most because it gave him the greatest pleasure.

A strangled sound poured from him. He pulled his mouth free and struggled for air. "I'm really trying to be a gentleman like you want, but I'm about to die here."

He needed to be inside her. Once she'd finished her duties at work, Heather had googled questions about virgins being deflowered. The information was mainly from romance novels with a few clinical articles mixed in. She'd read as many romances as she could and used the one phrase that was in each. "Fill me."

Warmth and passion radiated from him. A smile danced in his eyes. "You're so beautiful."

As long as he thought so, that's all she cared about. "Not as much as you."

His loud laughter competed with the music. The candles nearest them flickered. "I thought good fairies couldn't lie."

"I'm not. You're amazing."

Pure pleasure swept over his face, making him even better looking. He kissed her gently and positioned himself between her legs. "Ready?"

"For anything."

Daemon arched one eyebrow. "You tell me if you want to stop and I'll do my level best to try. If I can't, just kick me in the balls or my head."

"No. Never." That would be mean. "I won't want you to stop."

He hugged her with tenderness and affection.

That, more than anything, gave Heather the courage to relax.

He touched his cock to her opening and bathed the crown in her slick heat.

She liked that.

He eased a bit of the head inside.

That was good, too.

He sank farther into her.

A sharp pain stabbed through her sheath. She sucked in air.

Daemon froze. "We still good?"

She nodded. No lie. They always would be. She simply needed to get through this. "Maybe you should go fast."

"You're so tight. I don't want to hurt you."

"You won't."

"Sure?"

"Yes, please, just do it."

He plunged into her, stretching, owning, loving.

The pain peaked and faded, replaced by warmth she couldn't describe. Better than a kiss. More comforting than a caress. Crazy good. "Don't stop."

"Okay." He tunneled deeper, intent on her taking his full length inside.

It wasn't easy. She lifted her hips and pulled back her knees to give him greater access to what they both wanted.

His curls touched hers. His sac tapped against her buttocks.

She panted at the intense pressure in having him fill her. Whoever had written those novels she'd read hadn't made love with a former satyr. This was epic.

He heaved in a breath. "Doing okay?"

"Oh, yeah." Never had she been as warm, felt as close to another person or as loved. "Better than you can imagine."

They shared a smile that belonged to no one else except them. Nothing could match its power.

Daemon sank to his elbows, brushed his lips over hers and pumped lazily, nearly pulling his shaft from her before burrowing it back inside.

The resistance between their sexes generated a curious feeling, pleasant yet maddening.

He looked at her expectantly.

That beat everything else and was the best gift he could have given her. Him caring what she thought. "I'm all right. Don't stop."

He didn't, nor did he increase his pace. He took her carefully and gently, rubbing her clit as he slid in and out.

Her sheath seemed to grow narrower, or maybe he'd gotten thicker. In the end, it didn't matter. The friction delivered incomparable delight, followed by rapture. She invited the precious feeling closer, allowing it to grow in intensity and erase thoughts concerning good and bad.

That left only pleasure.

She surrendered to her release and the end of her virginity.

Chapter Six

The beast in Daemon wanted Heather in every possible way, his insatiable cock pounding into her narrow cunt and his hard kisses bruising her soft mouth as he proved his power over her. Plunging, thrusting and pumping with the impossible hunger he felt.

Yet, here he was, behaving better than a gentleman. His shaft's unhurried slide within her pussy wasn't that different from how she wanted him to eat. Taking one tiny bite at a time with no satisfying belch at the end.

He wanted to howl at the insanity of it but didn't. The man in him needed to concentrate on her enjoyment rather than his own.

He was so screwed.

His head fell forward. He breathed hard.

Her pussy contracted around his rod, proof she'd had a powerful orgasm.

Despite this slow torment, he puffed with pride, feeling more virile than when he'd had twenty nymphs in one night. A record in Couturie and a necessary fuckfest to prove he was *the man* to maintain his status in the forest.

Here, only Heather mattered. He'd gone through endless shit to get her place looking as nice as it did. He would have walked on broken toes and legs, if necessary, to give her everything he could.

He liked her. Hell, he needed her more than he wanted to admit but couldn't dwell on sappy stuff now.

She cupped his face in her achingly soft palms and stroked his cheeks. "Are you all right?"

His balls were about to blow, his cock so desperate for release pain shot down his thighs. "Fine."

She tightened her cunt around his rod, sucking him deeper inside.

His heart stalled then banged against his throat. "*Ah.*"

"What?"

Struggling for restraint, he gripped the sheets. "I need a minute."

"For what?"

To keep from crying. Even the agony he'd experienced from Becca's potion hadn't been this trying. He gritted his teeth and shook his head.

Heather worked her fingers through his hair. "Do you need to…to…"

She couldn't bring herself to say come. Daemon couldn't speak at all. He nodded vigorously.

"I'll help." She flexed her inner muscles and cupped his balls.

He just about screamed. "No. Stop." If she didn't, he might surrender to his beast and harm her without meaning to. "I'm trying not to lose control."

"Why?"

"I don't want to hurt you."

Heather fondled his boys. "You won't. Do your thing. Enjoy yourself."

If he really let loose, she might need Zoe to pry him off her. Sweat poured down his face and chest. He panted. "If I get too randy, claw my balls."

"No. I could never do anything so horrible."

Yet, she could kill him with foreplay. "It's all right." Even if she pulverized his damn nuts, she could heal them later. "Hang on."

He drove into her with a fury that was exquisitely satisfying and totally selfish. Which proved he was a mega prick and should slow down. He couldn't. The mattress jostled so much that pillows fell to the floor and the bedframe creaked. Heather's breasts shimmied like nobody's business. Her hair swished over the slippery sheets.

Each time he plowed deep inside and drove his shaft to the hilt, they smacked against each other, the sounds totally badass. When he pulled away, her pussy tightened, trying to drag him back inside.

For a good fairy, she was fucking wicked.

He pumped in time to the music's frenzied beat but hungered for more. Heaving air, he lifted her legs over his shoulders.

She squeaked and gripped his forearms.

Any harder and she'd bruise him. "You all right?"

"Uh-huh." She forced down a swallow. "Just holding on."

A wise move. He thrust into her repeatedly, spellbound at his rigid cock disappearing between her puffy folds. Shocking delight raced up his spine and down his belly, at last centering in his groin. His balls ached and his cock screamed for release.

Heather stopped digging her nails into his arms and caressed them instead. Her response told Daemon she was okay with what he was doing.

Overwhelmed with emotion, he pounded into her but also stroked her clit, his touch light and gentle.

She shuddered, growled in an unladylike manner and shrieked her release.

If he lived a thousand years, he'd never forget that beautiful noise. His climax slammed into him with such force he celebrated with a raucous howl, freeing his beast, reveling in his pulsing cock shooting cum into her.

Her face was red. His felt purple. They trembled, their smiles wobbly.

He struggled to speak. "I gotta…I gotta…"

She stared. "What?"

Before Daemon could tell her he needed to collapse, his arms and legs gave out. He sagged down. Her pebbled nipples poked his pecs. Liking that, he licked her thumb, to thank her as a gentleman would, gave her a deep, wet, longing kiss and passed out.

* * * *

Bitchin' good scents from cooked meat, garlic and grilled onions awakened him. He pushed to his elbows, surprised at the feast Heather had laid out on their bed. Steaks and prime rib sizzled with heat. Their pink juices told him she'd cooked them rare, as he'd seen on the Food Network while she'd been working. Cheese bubbled on the pizza topped with pepperoni and sausage, similar to the commercials he'd watched. Next to it were plates heaped with other stuff he recognized from TV—potato salad, coleslaw, deli meat and cheeses, bowls holding chips, both potato and corn.

No booze, though.

Daemon figured he shouldn't ask her about it. "How long was I out?"

"Enough for me to fix dinner." She cradled his face and stroked his lower lip in time to the earthy music. "You were beat."

He cuffed her wrist. "Did the pizza guy come back?"

Heather blinked. "No. I bought the pizza at the grocery store."

"Then why did you get dressed?" She'd put on her long white bathrobe. Daemon slipped his hand beneath the edge. She had her blouse and jeans on, too. "You feeling uncomfortable?"

"Only once we stopped." She smiled weakly. "While we were at it, I was fine."

"Tell you what. Get naked and we'll smear food over each other, eat it off then go at it again."

Even in the candlelight, her complexion darkened. Same as her mood.

She wasn't a free spirit by any means, but Daemon had never seen her so serious. His belly twisted. "Tell you what. We can eat the conventional way. That is, I can. One teeny, tiny bite at a time. At least one chew for each mouthful. No belching. Promise."

Heather smiled uncertainly. "I thought it'd be different."

His gut cramped. "What?" Fucking? Liking him? Wanting him to stay here?

She gestured to the bed.

He guessed she meant sex.

She lowered her face. "I hoped losing my virginity would make me bold."

"You had me blasting off just fine. I passed out, didn't I?"

"I envy you." She held his hand in hers. "I'm too timid."

"Take off your clothes and we'll fix that."

She stroked his palm, making his teeth tingle. "Is there more to what men and women do together than what we did?"

It'd take him months to detail everything he knew. He caressed her fingers. "Are you asking because you're curious or because it scares you?"

"Both. What else do lovers do with each other?"

"The regular stuff or kink?"

She recoiled.

"Hey." He squeezed her hand. "We don't have to talk about it. It's all right."

"No, it's not. I hate being the way I am." She tried to frown but couldn't quite manage it and drooped. "All my life, I've worried what others thought. No matter how much I want something, I always deny myself. I can't count the times I would have liked more than one Milky Way but told myself, 'Oh, no, you can't do that. There are poor fairies all over the world who can't afford even one candy bar. How dare you be so selfish?'"

"Are you kidding? Selfish is what your adoptive parents do. My guess is, they'd snatch candy from a baby."

"We're not talking about them. This is about me." She squared her shoulders. "Just once, I'd like to be like you. Free. Uninhibited. Uncivilized. Crude."

Daemon stopped scratching his ass. "Hold that thought."

"Where are you going?"

"Kitchen." He limped to it, grabbed what he'd tossed in the microwave earlier and hobbled back. "Here."

He offered her three Milky Ways.

Tears filled her eyes.

He'd hoped the candy would make her happy. "You want pizza instead? Steak? Prime rib?" He gestured to their fare. "Take it all. Please." If he had to, he'd eat the plants in her courtyard or he'd starve to keep her from crying.

She held his hand to her cheek. "I'm not hungry. Food isn't what I need."

Now, she was talking. He slipped his other hand beneath her robe and blouse.

"No, no, no." She dug her nails into his wrist. "I don't want to play."

There was no pleasing her, though he'd try. "Not a prob. However, a simple 'no' is fine. No need to rip me to shreds."

She released him. "I'm so sorry. Crud, I'm always sorry. I'm never normal."

"I hate to bring this up..." Especially when she was in such a snit. "But define normal."

"What you are when it comes to being physical with a woman. What else?" She dropped to the mattress.

Chips fell from bowls. Plates rattled against each other.

He wasn't going to call her on it. Even if the food ended up soaked into the mattress, he'd suck it out. "Baby, being oversexed isn't what it's cracked up to be."

She swiped away her tears. "That's not true and you know it. You've always had fun. I haven't. Even when I try, like you and I just did, I end up feeling guilty."

He sat and gathered her to him. "Once you get the hang of things, it'll get easier, I swear."

"I don't want to wait." She pulled away. "I want to be that way now. I wish I—"

"No, stop right there." Daemon gave her his hardest frown. "Don't ever say that again."

She crossed her arms. "Why? Because I'm a girl and I'm supposed to be nice and all that stuff guys think females should be?"

Good God, now she was accusing him of being politically correct. Becoming a simple satyr again was beginning to look good. "No. I was talking about making a wish. Remember what Becca said about being careful what you ask for?"

"You think I don't really want this? Or that I'm doomed to be nice?"

"Aw, babe." He slipped his hand beneath her robe and touched her boob. "Nice isn't bad."

"Honestly? Why don't you try it?" She pushed his hand away from her nipple. "I wish—"

He growled. "No, you don't. You have no idea what to wish for or what you'd be getting yourself into if it was granted. The problems you'd be bringing on yourself."

She threw up her hands. "Having fun with you would be a problem?"

"It's not that simple."

"Why not?"

He shoved his fingers through his hair, wanting to tear it out. "I didn't want to have to tell you this."

She grew quiet. Her eyes brimmed with new tears.

"Hey, hey, hey. No need to cry. This isn't about you. It's about me."

"I know." She hung her head and made a sound like she was dying inside. "You're married, aren't you? You have kids."

He laughed. "No."

Her gaze slid to his. "You don't want to stay with one woman? You don't want a family?"

How in the hell had they gotten on this subject? "Let me start over. Have you ever heard of Jinn?"

She covered her eyes. "You want another drink? The beer you had last night wasn't enough?"

"Not gin, like the booze." He would have killed for a shot right now. "Jinn. J-I-N-N."

Heather went blank.

"Another word for jinn is genie. You know, Aladdin, the magic lamp and all that. Is any of this ringing a bell?"

"I've read the story. What does that have to do with..." She inhaled sharply. "You have a genie?"

"Jinni." He held up his right middle finger.

Heather made a face. "Are you making an obscene gesture because I mispronounced the word?"

"I'm showing you my ring. No, don't touch it." He pulled his hand away. "You don't want to ever rub the stone. Promise me you won't, especially when I'm asleep or unconscious."

"Unconscious from what?"

Several zombies, if he was lucky. "Hitting my head or having another kind of accident, you know. I'm not the most graceful guy around. I want your word."

"I can't give it if I don't know the full extent of what I'd be agreeing to or why."

He sagged. "You don't trust me?"

"Sure, I do, when you're not putting on an act like now."

She was beginning to know him too well. "Fine." He straightened. "Ask away. I'll answer, even if it kills me."

"It won't get that far. I'll heal whatever hurts. Does your genie — jinni live in your ring?"

"Until I rub the stone. Before you ask anything else, let me show you something." Daemon pushed his hand between the mattress and box spring, searching for the damn notes he'd written earlier. He pulled them out, smoothed the pages and showed Heather what he'd scrawled on the sheets. Since it was in Satyr, his first language before he'd learned English, she couldn't possibly read it. "What you're looking at are the plans I made for when you came home tonight. All this." He gestured to the magnificent room, a feat he never thought he'd live to see. "Knowing MJ, I had to be very careful not to — "

"Wait. The same MJ you've mentioned before? He's your jinni?"

"She. Mistress Jin to be precise. She prefers MJ." He made a gagging noise. "Remember those bushes that were around your TV this morning?"

"She did that? Because she misses Couturie?"

He laughed and sobered quickly. "She likes to screw with my head. I wanted a beer to go with the pizza."

Heather gave him a disapproving look.

"Hey, don't blame me. Pizza and beer is practically a religion. When you fell asleep, I called on MJ and asked her for a Busch." He spelled it like the brewery did.

Confusion flooded Heather's face. "She misunderstood?"

"Like hell. I told her I wanted a beer, a Busch, to be precise. Up pops a Miller Light, which she knows I hate, along with the mini arboretum. A beer and a bush, get it? Ha-ha. I wasn't certain when you'd wake up, so I told her to nix the Miller for Coors."

"Maybe she doesn't want you to drink, either."

He hung his head and breathed hard. "Ah, hon, she's not like that. She delights in torturing me. Did the same with her last Master, the guy I fought in Couturie. Remember me mentioning him?" Daemon didn't wait for her answer. "Once I beat his ass, he not only welcomed me with open arms, he gave me his ring. I thought, 'Hey, I'm the man now'. Yeah, right. The SOB couldn't wait to get rid of it."

"You can't give it back?"

"Fucking thing won't come off." He sagged to the mattress next to the prime rib. It smelled awesome, but he didn't dare chow down with this business unsettled and risk Heather having another meltdown. "You cannot believe the crap I've gone through with MJ. Just getting this place to look as rocking as it does now was a major effort, even with these." He lifted the papers. "I wasn't sure if the stuff on the walls were called panels, curtains, drapes or something else, so I told MJ to cover it with silk fabric. I mean really, who could misunderstand that?" He rolled his eyes. "She plastered the place with bras, panties and negligees made of silk fabric, like this was a lingerie store or something. By the way, according to your TV, Victoria's Secret is having a sale this weekend.

"Anyway, once I straightened out the silk panel fiasco, getting the music was a monumental bitch. I told her it should only play in this room, that I didn't want anyone outside to hear it since you're not tight with your neighbors. Again, easy to understand. She made the people next door deaf. The guy ran outside screaming that something was wrong with his ears."

Heather clutched his hand in hers. "Are he and his wife okay now?"

"Yeah. MJ finally got that right."

"Did she make anything else go wrong on them?" Heather drew in her shoulders. "Will I have to touch him and her so they heal?"

"Not to worry." Daemon patted her fingers. "They're good now." Or at least he hoped. He blew out a breath. "Back to me. When I first decided I wanted to look totally human, I made the mistake of wishing for my tail, horns and hooves to go away. I mean, if you can't use your personal jinni for that, what good is she, right? My damn horns and tail started to go away, or rather leave the vicinity in opposite directions, pulling me with them to the left and to the right. My legs took off in a sprint without me attached to them. They were halfway through the forest before one of my friends tackled the damn things and dragged them back. That's when I decided to seek professional help at your place."

He paused to swallow and drag in more air. "Getting the cash for my treatment was un-fucking-believable. I actually drew MJ a picture of what the bills should look like. Mortals are always losing their wallets in the forest, so I knew what I needed. Guess what I got. A stack of bills that were identical to my drawing. I finally found a five-dollar bill that a tourist had lost and showed it to her, insisting the rest of the currency look precisely like it. I got five thousand of those suckers all with the same serial numbers that I figured your company's bank would notice when you went to deposit them. I may not have lived in the mortal world, but I have been paying attention to how it works, mainly from TV shows I watch on smartphones humans lose. *Quantico* and *Blindspot* are the best. The babes in that are fucking hardcore. Finally, I told MJ to bring me all the lost US currency in the French Quarter. Bills that fell out of people's pockets or they'd left somewhere. I'm no thief. Within seconds, I had a stack taller than I am. Money along with throwaway flyers also known as bills. Took me days to separate the good stuff from the crap. You don't want to ask her for anything. Ever."

Heather ran her fingers over his. "I'm sorry it's been so difficult for you."

Her words were a balm, her touch the best magic. Sorcery and wishes could never match its power. Tension drained from him. He smiled.

"However…"

His smile wilted. "What?"

"Did you ever think she's that way because you're a guy? Her Master, you said. That sounds medieval. She'd probably be different with another woman, especially a good fairy who's non-threatening."

"Uh-uh. No way. She'd eat you alive." Before Heather could touch his ring, he snatched his hand back and pushed to a sitting position. "I've already told you, she likes to play with my head. That would mean screwing you over royally, since you've never dealt with her. Technically, you don't even have the power to get a wish, but I'd lay bets she'd give you one just to stick it to me. I don't want you to change. You're fine as you are. I like you sweet."

"Even though I don't? Even though it makes me feel guilty whenever we have uh…uh…"

She was going to kill him. "The word is sex. And we'll work on that. A lot. Promise." Teaching her everything he knew would be a privilege.

"Are you and MJ lovers?"

He went clammy then hot. His heart pumped faster than the music.

"That's what I thought." Heather lowered her face, her manner small rather than accusing.

Daemon wished she'd bitched at him. Her anger would have made this easier. "Heather…"

"No, I understand if you don't want me to meet MJ because you're sleeping with her."

"Was. Not now. Hell, before I met you, I slept with everyone."

She shot him a decidedly nasty look.

Daemon started over. "She'll turn your life upside down."

"Maybe that's what I need. Is she into ki…ki…ki…ki…" Unable to get the word out, Heather whimpered. "Is MJ into it?"

Was she ever. He rubbed his temple. "Ah…"

She touched his cheek. "Do you like it, too?"

He got brave and met her gaze. She wasn't crying, thank God, but she looked lost and sad. Probably the same way she'd been when her adoptive parents had thrown her out for being too good. Pricks.

Daemon figured she worried about him getting tired of her and ordinary sex when there was so much more out there. He wanted to say that wouldn't happen but he wasn't sure. His feelings for Heather and how she kept burrowing into his heart scared him badly. He wanted to bolt, yet couldn't move. Someday, he might be able to do so and could possibly run like hell, breaking her heart which would pulverize his. "I'd like to try everything with you."

She cupped his face. "Please have her make me wild like you are."

"Not that wild." He preferred to run the show, chasing Heather down and having her submit, not the other way around. All he needed was her surrendering to pleasure with endless enthusiasm, no guilt. "You're sure you can't do this by yourself? You know, overcome your natural tendency to make everything a problem?"

"Do I do that?"

"It's your nature, babe."

She chewed her nail. "Maybe MJ's my only hope. We should get her out here."

"Not so fast." He pushed her hand away before she could rub the stone. "We need to know exactly what you're going to ask for before you say one word."

"Okay. How do you suggest I say I want to be wild, though not as much as you?"

"Carefully. Otherwise, she could turn you into a female version of the Abominable Snowman — saw that on TV this afternoon. To her, it would be something wild with fewer muscles than I have."

Heather sagged to the bed.

Feeling bad, Daemon slapped a Milky Way in her hand. She finished it quickly and was peeling the wrapper from the second one when she stopped and looked appalled.

"Finish it. It'll be good practice for being bad." He pulled the prime rib closer. "We can figure this out while we eat."

"Is she able to hear what we're saying?"

Daemon had never considered the possibility. He twisted his ring so the stone faced his palm. For good measure, he made a fist, hopefully soundproofing her digs.

Once he'd polished off the prime rib and steaks, he dove into the deli meats and even belched several times. Heather didn't scold. Either she no longer cared how crudely he behaved, his personal choice, or she was too busy with how to express her wish. After eating her third chocolate bar, she looked green around the edges.

He warned her again about MJ twisting whatever she'd ask for. "Believe me, she's an expert at that."

"Are you saying I shouldn't even mention the word kiss?"

"Not unless you want that old rock band in here looking as they do now, wrinkled and ugly."

"We better write this down."

They shared the pizza as they brainstormed. After they finished the potato salad, cheeses, coleslaw and chips, Daemon grabbed the Cool Ranch Doritos from the freezer. "How do we cook these?"

"Ah, since they're frozen when they shouldn't be, you can put them in the microwave for a few seconds to thaw them."

What came out wasn't pretty. Daemon finished the soggy wad, anyway, and read Heather's wishes, each written in a perfect script, no going outside the lines. Poor girl had to loosen up. "The first one's too vague. Telling her you'd like to be good at sex will probably get you a one-way ticket to a Vegas brothel."

"What?" Color stained her cheeks. "I'm so embarrassed."

"No need to be. This is simply your learning curve." He scanned her notes and shook his head. "Wishing for you to be good at sex with me is better, but still not narrow enough. I swear, she'll have us performing in a triple X-rated show either at a club or in a sex flick."

"Maybe I shouldn't mention sex at all, but something else like a once-in-a-lifetime romance with my soulmate."

Warning bells sounded. The old Daemon would have bolted. The new him couldn't do anything but stick close, entranced by her softness, heat and scent. "As nice as that sounds, if she knows about Keremend and Sylvania, we could both end up dead."

"Who are they?"

"The satyr version of Romeo and Juliet."

Heather covered her face. "This is too hard."

Tell him something he didn't know. He read further and tapped the second to last wish. "This is pretty good. You've made it narrow enough with endless explanations in between that she can't possibly screw it up."

"Unless she likes defying you."

That was true.

"Have you ever punished her for deliberately getting stuff wrong?"

Their best times together involved those sexy-as-hell punishments. Daemon's face burned. He cleared his throat and brought the empty plates to the kitchen. "Let's concentrate on you. Are you ready to meet her?"

Heather pushed off the bed, pulled the robe more snugly around herself and tightened the belt. "Sure."

He tottered to her side. "If this goes bad, can you heal yourself?"

She stared. "No. We'd have to call another good fairy in or have Becca make a potion, if there is one for something like this."

"Maybe we shouldn't do this then. I've lived through Becca's potions. Barely."

"We could call her mom. Rowena's the best and she won't let us down. Please, I have to try. I need to start taking chances."

Brave words from a good fairy who hadn't seen MJ in action. Once she had, maybe that would convince her to change without the jinni's help or wallow in guilt for her remaining days.

Daemon bet on the latter choice. "Okay. Let's do it. Sit over there." He pointed to the farthest corner in the kitchen.

"If I'm on the floor behind the counter, MJ won't be able to see me from here."

"Exactly. I want to test her out before we get into your wish. See if she's in a good mood."

"If she's not?"

"Run like hell. Don't worry about me. Once I get her back in the stone, your healing or Becca's or her mom's potions can take care of whatever she screwed up on me."

Heather took his hand. "No. We're doing this together."

Sounded nice and downright foolish.

She kissed his knuckles. "Ready?"

Not for this. Never for this. Daemon nodded reluctantly and touched the stone. Heather put her finger on his. Together, they drew the first circle.

She pressed against him. "Don't you say anything?"

"Only a prayer in my head that this isn't the hugest fucking mistake of my life. Other than that, no."

"Let's do it."

They drew the second circle.

She tensed. "How many more?"

"One."

They completed it.

Every candle blew out. The music paused. A flash brighter than lightning lit up the area. Iridescent smoke filled the room, the plumes bright red and orange, resembling the lava he'd seen on TV today.

The candles sputtered to life again, along with the sensual beat. The smoke cleared.

Heather gasped.

Chapter Seven

Talk about opening the proverbial can of worms.

Given what Daemon had said about MJ, Heather had expected major trouble and predicted the jinni would be a cross between John Goodman in *10 Cloverfield Lane*, a truly frightening film, and Hannibal Lecter in *Silence of the Lambs*, an equally troubling movie with no lambs whatsoever.

MJ didn't resemble either maniac. This was way, way worse and made Heather's stomach cramp. In the looks department, MJ beat the babe who'd turned Daemon's head on the street. She was possibly early twenties in human years, her features exotic. Wavy black hair dangled past her waist. In the candlelight, her caramel-colored skin appeared unbelievably rich.

Next to that, Heather's complexion looked like the undead and was about as appealing. The same went for her figure.

MJ's curves were decidedly voluptuous. She was at least a C-cup, with lush hips and long legs made for a man's lust.

When Daemon had advised her to be careful what to wish for, Heather had taken him seriously, though clearly not enough. She should have fled but couldn't. This was like watching a train wreck.

MJ's bra and thong, if Heather could call them that, consisted of delicate gold chains that twinkled in the room's soft glow and barely covered her nipples and mound. Slave bracelets with tiny bells hugged her biceps and ankles.

She stretched, catlike. The way one would when pulled from a satisfying sleep. Her bells tinkled.

Daemon sighed. Thankfully, it sounded more dismayed than aroused.

MJ opened her eyes.

Heather forgot to breathe. Her irises were violet. To say they were stunning didn't adequately describe them.

MJ offered Daemon a slow, sensuous smile. "Hey, baby."

The smoke in her voice, its raw sexual allure, was like nothing Heather had ever heard, not even from Satan. Something within her fluttered and her cheeks warmed. If the jinni had such an unexpected effect on her, what must she be doing to Daemon?

He mumbled something vaguely nasty, rather than turned on, and said no more, possibly scared to have it misinterpreted.

Smiling, MJ padded to him and ground her hips against his, her pussy to his shaft.

Heather couldn't believe such outrageous behavior and in her own home, no less. She bristled.

"Uh-uh." Daemon backed away from MJ. "How about you stand over there as we talk?" He jabbed his thumb at the kitchen.

She dragged her big toe up his calf.

Heather gritted her teeth so hard they hurt.

"You want to talk?" MJ purred. "You're ready to get rid of those ugly feet and let me get you some better-looking ones?"

"Okay, that is it. I'm sorry, but it is." Heather tapped MJ's shoulder to get her attention. "His feet are more beautiful than Eric's or anyone else's, even yours."

That was saying a lot. MJ's feet were spectacular, feminine and narrow. She'd painted her toenails a glittery gold.

She took in Heather with mild surprise that said she'd just noticed her. "Hey, there."

Her voice was even huskier and naked with desire.

Heather clutched her bathrobe to her throat and stepped back.

"Whoa." Daemon grabbed MJ's arm to stop her from following. "Stay here. Got it?"

"Yes, Master." She rubbed her boobs against his chest.

He pried her off him and held her at arm's length, his hand on her shoulder. "Stay there."

"Yes, Master." She ran her fingers down his arm to his pit and played with the silky hair.

Daemon twisted away and glanced at Heather. "See what I meant about…" He inclined his head to MJ.

Heather got his drift but recalled something else he'd said earlier. "Is this for real or is she putting you on? You know, playing with your head?"

Surprise flashed on MJ's face. Vulnerability, too, that went soul deep. She hid both reactions quickly. "Hmm, let me guess." She stalked to Heather. "With all the white you're wearing, you must be a good fairy. Yet, something's off." She wiggled her eyebrows at Daemon. "The eagle has landed for this one, right?"

Heather covered her face.

Daemon sniffed. "None of your business."

"I'm only trying to help. What's the matter, Precious?" She stroked Heather's hair. "You didn't enjoy boogieing with Daemon?"

Heather wished she could lie. That would have made this much easier. She looked to Daemon for help.

MJ sashayed to him. "You brought me out because you've lost your touch with the ladies and want it back?"

"No. Never. He's perfect." Heather pulled her robe more tightly around herself. "It's me who's messed up."

"Like hell." Daemon smiled softly. "You're amazing."

MJ gave them both an indulgent smile. "Maybe I'm the one who needs a change."

Daemon glared at her. "If I could take the ring off, I would. I've already told you that. And, no, I'm not setting you loose on the world. There's already war, famine, Ebola... No one needs more shit than they already have."

"In that case, my job here is done." She gestured to his ring. "Stuff me back inside my teeny-tiny cell. The next episode of *Suits* is coming on in five. Looks like Louis is about to screw up again. I don't want to miss it."

"Wait." Heather approached cautiously. "I'm not making a wish. I just want to ask a question, all right?"

MJ moistened her lips slowly, seductively.

Heather had never witnessed anything as mesmerizing. Maybe MJ could teach her stuff like that to please Daemon and they could forego this wish business. "Do that again."

Bewilderment rose in MJ's eyes. "What?"

"The thing with your lips. Does that come naturally to you or is it something you learned?"

"Depends. Do you actually expect me to answer your question?"

Daemon bumped her shoulder with his. "Cut the 'tude."

She arched one dark eyebrow. "As you wish, my most glorious Master." After an elaborate bow, she spoke to Heather. "What was your question again?"

"Does that—wait, I'm forgetting my manners." Heather touched Daemon's arm. "So are you."

"What are you talking about? I haven't belched once since she got here and I don't have to cover my cock. She's already seen it countless times."

This couldn't get worse. "That's not what I meant." She offered her hand to MJ. "Daemon forgot to introduce us. Hi, I'm Heather."

"Hey, there, Precious. What's your question?"

Even her adoptive parents weren't that direct and they had no social skills whatsoever. "The way you act, licking your lips and stuff, are you putting on? Or is that your real personality? In either case, is that something you could teach me?"

"That's several questions and I don't teach. I do."

Daemon shook his head.

MJ smiled. "Am I out here for a reason or has everyone run out of wishes?"

For once, Heather didn't want to be nice or grovel. Her future with Daemon depended upon her being bold. "Forget the wish stuff for a minute. I have another question first and I expect an answer. Please. In your expert opinion, is it possible to make a good fairy wild?"

"Hold it." Daemon pulled Heather back. "What she means is sexually uninhibited without any guilt, right?" He shot Heather a look that said she hadn't narrowed her question enough.

This was worse than *Jeopardy*. "Yeah. What he said."

"You want to be sexually wild without me granting a wish to that effect?"

Nothing could be more perfect. "Would it be possible?"

"Depends on what I can get out of it."

Heather got tough. "Not Daemon. Never Daemon."

He gave her a puppy-dog look along with a sweet smile.

She returned it.

"So, he's off-limits." MJ tapped her chin. "How about you?" She edged closer.

Daemon yanked MJ back. "You're going to do this without anyone wishing for it?"

"Sure. I can teach Precious everything she needs to know about carnal pleasure without the nasty guilt." MJ raked her gaze over her. "I'll enjoy her lessons. Probably more than she does."

Sweat ran down Heather's back. She tried to swallow but the lump in her throat wouldn't allow it. "Huh?"

Daemon shrugged. "As long as a wish isn't involved, I'm good with it."

She couldn't believe he'd said that.

MJ nodded. "I do have a request before I begin."

Heather backed away from them both. "Don't I get a say in this?"

Daemon fumed at MJ. "You have a request? Yeah, right. Whatever it is, the answer's no."

"I just want a little time out of my cell, that's all. I'm not asking for a trip to Paris with Adam Levine."

"I would hope not." Heather gave her a scolding look. "He's married and has a baby. A precious little girl."

Daemon clenched his jaw. "How much time?"

She stroked his broad chest and dipped her fingers to his groin.

Heather rushed to them. "Hey. None of that in my place." Especially with her guy.

MJ ignored her. "I want in on the action between you two, every decadent minute of it, teaching Precious what she doesn't know. While I'm working my magic, you can watch, participate, whatever butters your biscuit. Deal?"

"No." Heather had never been so appalled and strangely aroused. "This is so wrong."

Daemon scratched his jaw. "Which oddly enough makes it right. It is a way for you to get what you want without risking a wish." He spoke to MJ. "You don't grant her any wishes, got it?"

"Are you wishing for that?"

He crowded her with his far-bigger body. Height-wise, she was on a par with Heather.

MJ smiled agreeably. "Your non-wish is my command."

"Babe?" He looked at Heather expectantly. "You in? Whatever you choose, I'll support you."

Until he got tired of her moods shooting up and down like a yo-yo. Guilt was driving Heather crazy. She felt foolish around experienced lovers like him and MJ. They accepted life for what it was, natural, uncomplicated and simply a good time, while she troubled over everything. It was long past due for her to grow up and be as uninhibited as they were. "Sure." She cleared the tremor from her throat. "Let's do it."

Mischief and lust filled MJ's eyes. She approached and cradled Heather's fingers.

Her breath caught at the tender move. Rather than scoot away, Heather leaned in.

Pleasure filled MJ's lovely face. "You want me to teach you everything I know?"

That sounded kind of awful, yet intriguing, too. "Ah, the simple things first, please. Like your lip stuff."

"That comes naturally after you know how to seduce a man."

Heather laughed. "I'll never be able to do that."

"You wouldn't be putting me on now, would you?"

Daemon plopped on the bed and massaged his toes. "Good fairies can't lie. Right, babe?"

She nodded.

MJ pried Heather's hand from the robe. "Let's start by getting rid of this."

Daemon made a frustrated sound. "There's more beneath it."

Compassion, rather than amusement, filled MJ's eyes. Another surprise Heather hadn't expected given how MJ behaved and looked. "Thanks...for taking it easy with me."

"Don't you worry. I'll be far gentler with you than he's been."

"Hey. I've been a perfect gentleman. No belching. No showing my cock to pizza guys. No eating fast even if I'm starving."

Heather offered a wan smile. "He has been good."

MJ eased Heather's blouse and bra off with loving care.

Nice. Heather's head lolled back.

MJ changed the music to a softer, subtler beat, more appropriate for a timid fairy.

The mattress squeaked beneath Daemon. "Will Behemoth be next?"

"Care to wish for it?"

He fell silent.

MJ sank to her knees and carefully removed Heather's jeans and panties.

Her arousal grew. Already Daemon's presence had dampened her curls and plumped her delicate folds. She inhaled deeply.

"Easy." MJ stroked Heather's hip. "I'll never hurt you."

I know. MJ wasn't anything like Daemon had claimed, her badass jinni nothing more than an act. Heather cupped her chin. "You've had it hard, haven't you?"

Pain flared in her exquisite eyes. She shrugged.

Empathy flooded Heather. "I'm so sorry."

"Ladies?" Daemon didn't sound pleased. "What's going on?"

Something inside MJ seemed to shift, her sorrow and compassion gone, the hardcore troublemaker returned. "Nothing." On her feet, she slipped her arm around Heather's waist. "Come on." Despite her new manner, she embraced Heather gently. "Time for some serious bed play, uber good and guilt-free."

Sounded good, except Heather couldn't shake off MJ's transformation so easily. She was the saddest person Heather had ever met. She ached for her and wished her healing powers could bring her happiness. Sadly, that wasn't possible. However, a good hug couldn't hurt. She halted and embraced MJ as she'd often done with Becca, Constance and even Zoe, despite how hot her skin was. An occupational hazard for a demon.

A chuckle spilled from MJ. It sounded forced. "What's this? You're hot for me now, too?"

The notion made Heather's cheeks sting. For her, a threesome wasn't possible. If MJ had leaned that way with other Masters or mortals, that was okay. Heather would never judge. "Not hot, interested in you as a friend." She spoke softly so Daemon couldn't overhear. "You're not alone anymore. Not as long as I'm around. You can count on me. Whenever you want to talk, just say the word. I'll listen."

MJ looked uneasy. "Why are you doing this?"

"I want to. You're a good person." An odd trait when she was also sexier than sin. Her skin smelled rich, heated and vibrant. The way a woman should, unless she was a good fairy. "Can we be friends?"

"Seriously?"

"Yeah. Remember, I can't lie. So can we?"

Her eyes grew moist. "Sure."

"Good. Because we are, please don't laugh at whatever I do. I'm new at this."

"Not for long." MJ brought her to the bed.

Daemon pushed off the mattress and ogled Heather as he had those near-naked babes in *Dancing with the Stars.*

"Down you go." MJ eased her to the mattress, spread her legs and positioned her arms above her head as today's sexual sacrifice, which she was. She giggled hysterically.

"Hey, babe." Daemon leaned over her, looking worried. "You all right?"

Heather loved him so much it hurt. She pressed her face to his chest, adoring his musky clean scent.

He stopped breathing.

She could have sniffed him for hours but her neck cramped and she fell back to the mattress. "I'm good."

He exchanged a loaded glance with MJ.

She positioned herself between Heather's legs. Daemon clasped her wrists, imprisoning them.

Her pulse jumped. "What are you teaching me now?"

"How to relax and ditch the guilt." MJ winked. "This is the only way, unless you want a wish."

"No." Heather and Daemon spoke as one.

"Roger that." She stroked Heather's inner thighs.

Heat and satisfaction washed over her.

Daemon rubbed her nose with his.

Wasn't nearly enough. She strained to reach him. Their lips touched. A jolt shot between them, more powerful than an electric current.

MJ eased two fingers inside Heather's channel and tongued her clit.

Her mouth fell open on a soundless but definitely guilty cry.

Daemon's tongue filled her quickly and completely, his kiss deep, on fire, pure male. The intimacy pushed away doubt, remorse and good sense.

MJ lapped Heather's folds with loving care then concentrated on her nub. She licked lightly and playfully.

Coupled with Daemon's astonishing kiss, carnal hunger built within Heather. Intolerable desire coiled in her belly, rushed down her legs and up her torso. She grew hypersensitive to each touch.

He fondled her breasts.

She struggled to get closer to him.

MJ slid her fingers in and out of Heather's sheath, a slow, sensuous taking. She sucked Heather's nub and gently probed her anus.

Heather gasped in delight.

Daemon quieted the sound with his tongue, his kiss intoxicating.

Pleasure intensified in her pussy and demanded its due.

MJ stilled her fingers and circled Heather's clit with her tongue, coming close but not quite touching it.

That was mean for a friend to do. She needed release.

Daemon didn't help. He kissed her hard one last time and pulled away.

Before Heather could catch her breath and ask what he was doing, he straddled her. His cock brushed her chin. Sex perfumed his rigid shaft.

Dutifully and wantonly, she eased his crown inside her mouth. There wasn't anything to match his salty pre-cum and wonderfully hot and silky flesh. She licked.

He shuddered. "More. Take all of me inside."

Nothing else will do.

MJ thumbed Heather's nub. Firm, fast strokes meant to send her to heaven and beyond. Euphoria burst through her. She trembled.

Daemon panted. "More."

She couldn't deny him, especially to wallow in her own pleasure. Falling in love precluded that. Even with MJ working her sex, Heather tended to Daemon's. A slave to pleasure that demanded yet gave, thrilled and soothed and banished all shame.

Each moment built upon the next. The music receded, replaced by sounds only lovers make. Soft moans, escalating sighs, words too quiet to hear and too breathless to understand.

Heather's climax punched through her with incredible force, deep and satisfying.

Daemon's loud roar followed.

She sucked him dry.

Spent, they panted and grinned at each other.

MJ crawled to Heather's side and eased her hair from her damp face. "How you doing?"

Not good. She felt selfish, another hang-up she had. There seemed no end to her flaws. "You didn't have any fun. That's not right. It's not fair." Unfortunately, Heather didn't know what to do about it unless she asked Daemon to see to MJ's pleasure.

Picturing them as lovers hurt deep and was a moot point.

Daemon's head hung between his shoulders, his lids slipped to half-mast. He listed to the right, ready to topple over.

"I'll take care of this." MJ shoved him.

His arms flailed. He muttered something and crashed to the mattress.

The bedframe shook and groaned.

Heather sat up. "You didn't have to be so rough."

"He's a big guy. He won't break. Now, about my fun." With a playful smile, she cupped Heather's neck and drew her closer.

The tiny bells on MJ's arm and ankle bands tinkled. Her breath smelled like cinnamon.

Heather's vision blurred. She couldn't breathe. Her heart walloped. "What are you doing?"

"Being friends like you wanted." Her sly smile said she was putting on.

Heather liked the real MJ better than the fake one. "You've been lonely, like I was, and you find it hard to trust. No reason to pretend otherwise or put on an act for me. Not like you do for Daemon."

Escape was written on her face. She shook it off. "Are you always this direct?"

"Sometimes friends have to be."

"Fine. I'm busted." She slouched. "Are you satisfied?"

"Oh, no." Heather cradled her face. "I wasn't being judgmental. I want to make you happy...within reason."

MJ slanted her a look. "Would another hug and maybe a massage be asking too much? I haven't had one in eons."

"Then it's time you did." Heather threw her arms around her, squeezed tightly and rocked them back and forth. "Lie down and I'll heal whatever hurts."

"My shoulders and neck are freaking killing me. It's hard to stand upright in the ring."

"That's terrible." She helped MJ to the comforter, brushed aside her golden chains and worked her magic on her shoulders. They were warm, soft and as perfect as her other parts.

"Whoo." She exhaled noisily. "That feels good. Don't stop."

Nothing would make her do so. Not even Daemon asking for attention. At this moment, MJ needed her more. "Have you always been a jinni or were you a mortal at one time? If you don't mind me asking."

"S'okay. My past is an open book to Daemon. He has my files. If he wants to tell you, I'm sure he will."

That didn't seem right. Jinns should have had the same privacy rights as everyone else. "I'd rather hear it from you."

She folded her arms beneath her head and released a sigh. "I was always a jinn. My Masters change but circumstances haven't. I've been stuck in the same ring for eons. Same as my parents."

"You have some?" Heather stroked MJ's back. Her light healing touch unknotted those muscles. "You all live in the same ring?"

Her laughter chimed through the room. "No. That would have been too crowded. Once I was born, I was sent to my first Master. The only time female and male jinns come together is to procreate. That usually lasts two weeks."

"How awful and sad, not to mention lonely."

"Hey, at least they have some fun before they have to go back to work."

"Uh…have you…are you…"

"A mom? Naw. I didn't want to do to a new jinni what happened to me. I'll fuck with any guy immortal or mortal, but jinns are out of the question."

She was a good person. Heather stroked her hair. "If you were newly born when you went to your first Master, did he have to like feed and diaper you until you grew up?"

More snickers. "The dude was so helpless he wouldn't have known how and wouldn't have wanted to learn. I was fully grown the moment I was born, housebroken and everything. I know that makes no sense, but what does when it comes to supernatural stuff?"

Heather had never thought of things that way. No wonder mortals considered paras strange. "From what you said, your first Master sounds kind of demanding."

"Had me hopping to round the clock."

"Wasn't he ever good to you? Thinking of your needs rather than his?"

"Thanks for the massage. It was great." She rolled to the side and pulled her knees to her chest.

The way Heather did when she was blue and needed to comfort herself. She longed to dispel MJ's unhappiness and cradled her shoulder. "What happened? You can tell me."

She swiped at her eyes. "I was a fool. Okay?"

"Why do you say that?"

"Because I worked morning, noon and night to make him happy. I thought if I gave him my all, he'd love me, or at least like me a little."

He hadn't. That truth was in her gorgeous eyes.

"He was a fool." Heather caressed her. "You deserve better. Did you meet any other guys you liked?"

"After him, I swore off love. My other Masters weren't too great, either. Now, I just want to screw. Keep things simple."

But empty. Heather wasn't about to argue. MJ had to do things in her own good time. Someday, she'd find a guy who'd love her as much as she needed. Possibly several dudes at once since she liked to mess around so much. "Would you like to keep talking?"

She sniffled. "Not about me. What's your story? You said you were lonely too. I don't buy it. You're beautiful and sweet and...well, you know."

Her praise touched Heather's soul. "I had a challenging childhood." She told her about the misunderstandings with her adoptive parents. "Like you, I tried everything I knew to please them, except for hurting mortals and stealing stuff. One year, I was so good I expected them to reward me with a really great Christmas gift like birth parents do with their kids."

"I'm guessing that didn't turn out too well. What did they get you?"

She lowered her face. "Nothing. They said if I wanted a present, there were plenty of kids in the neighborhood and I could snatch one from them."

"Aw, that's mean. Let's forget about them and the prick, or rather pricks, I had for Masters. Want to learn how to lick your lips like I do?"

"Sure."

MJ demonstrated.

Heather mimicked her. "That wasn't right, was it?"

"Only because you're overthinking it. Don't. Just do it. Again."

Daemon awakened.

Heather drew her tongue across her bottom lip at a lazy pace and partially closed her eyes.

He smiled, ate the remaining chips and belched.

Chapter Eight

Exhausted from the previous evening, Heather ducked into work five minutes later than usual, which meant she was only ten minutes early.

Zoe was waiting, grumpy as always. "Someone has an admirer."

Heather froze, certain her face gave away the depravity she and Daemon had indulged in last night with MJ helping to dispel the regret. An apology was on her lips for wanting more.

An overwhelming stench hit.

For once, it didn't come from Zoe.

Someone had put a pretty earthenware pot on Heather's desk. The plant in it had spiny green leaves and a fuzzy salmon-colored flower with petals shaped like a starfish. She stepped toward it and just about gagged at the odor.

"Carrion flower." Zoe clasped her hands to her throat. "My absolute fave. Like I said, you have an admirer. There's a card. Open it."

Heather held her breath and pulled the note from its small black envelope. Not recognizing the scrawl, she read,

Hoping today is better for you. Check your overdue accounts.
– S

The sentiment and appalling stink brought tears to Heather's eyes. She opened her spreadsheet and the company bank account. Satan had settled his overdue charges. What a sweetie.

Heather breathed through her mouth. Didn't help. Now she could taste the awful odor and tried not to heave. "Would you like the plant, since it's your favorite?"

"Totally. Thanks." Zoe hugged it to her scrawny chest and ran her nose against the fuzzy petals. Before she reached the hall, she halted and turned back.

Heather stopped spraying her talcum-powder cologne. She hid the atomizer behind herself, not wanting Zoe to feel bad. "What?" She hoped Zoe wasn't going to return the plant.

She approached fast, her saddle oxfords slapping the floor, her head thrust forward, eyes narrowed.

"I know you like the stench—the way the plant smells." Heather forced a smile. "It's just not my thing, so please don't misunderstand the cologne I sprayed. I'm not being judgmental. I'd never be that way. I hope you know as much. You're a demon, I'm a good fairy. We have different tastes. Please believe me."

Zoe made a face. "You're wearing makeup."

Only some Vaseline on her lips. They were swollen and sore from kissing Daemon so much. Recalling those moments, she went into a full-body blush.

Zoe shook her head and drifted down the hall, snuggling and cooing to her plant as a mortal would to a baby.

Constance strolled by next, stopped dead and gaped at Heather. "Oh, damn, girl. You didn't."

Her sexual corruption couldn't be that obvious. She fingered the neck on her white blouse and froze. She hadn't fastened the top button. A first for her.

Constance hurried to Heather's side and lifted her hands.

Heather backed into her chair. It rolled into the wall. "No, don't, please." She didn't want to lose her memories from last night.

"I'm not doing anything. Chill." Constance adjusted her turban. The hand-painted parrots and flowers on it were identical to those on her gown.

Heather remembered to breathe. "Beautiful outfit."

"Thanks." She leaned close. "How was he? No, wait, how are you? He's so damn big, I'm surprised you're still able to walk this morning. Are you okay? What did he do? What did you? Tell me every —"

"Guys..." Becca stared as hard as Constance and Zoe had.

Heather braced herself for a lecture.

Becca took Heather's hand in hers. "Are you all right?"

Unable to lie, she nodded and smiled, knowing no shame.

"Good." Becca slipped her arm through Constance's and tugged her toward the hall.

She held back. "What are you doing?"

"Leading you back to your office, where you belong."

"I'm on a break."

"Take it later. Away from Heather. She's an adult and can do what she wants without our interference or judgment."

"Who's judging?" Constance lifted her chin. "I simply want details."

Becca smiled at Heather. "Please take care of yourself. We're here for you, no matter what, okay?"

Constance called over her shoulder, "Let's do lunch. I'll buy."

Becca swore and pulled her away.

Heather waited until they rounded the corner before she checked herself in her pocket mirror. Dark smudges ringed her eyes thanks to too little sleep. Her mouth was bruised, her lips puffier than Angelina Jolie's. Three strands of hair were out of place. Her top button still undone.

No wonder they'd stared. She'd gone over to the Dark Side with scant effort. What was next? Showing up for work a minute late? Taking a half hour for lunch, rather than five minutes as she usually did, so she could race home and fall into Daemon's arms then share her terrible history with MJ as she'd shared hers? Strutting around her apartment naked, the same as them?

Daemon's nudity filled Heather's mind, exciting and daunting her.

She banished those images and got into her day. She sent a thank-you note to Satan, telling him how she loved his gesture. The truth. She was about to add an apology for how she'd behaved to him but didn't, sensing it would ring false.

She was a changed woman now. *Some might say a fallen one.*

Killing her pleased smile, she healed a poor vamp who'd spent several days there in their dark room. He was a new client, shaken from his treatment that banned blood sucking. If he wanted plasma, he had to drink it from a bottle like a civilized person. He'd become so frustrated, he'd sunk his teeth into his wrist. When he couldn't find any blood, he'd gone off the deep end and nearly chewed his hand off.

At lunch, Constance hurried to Heather's desk, her purse shoved beneath her arm. "Mickey D's McPick 2 menu is calling to me, how about you?"

Heather's stomach growled for a Quarter Pounder with Cheese.

"There you are." Becca gave Constance a reproving look.

She sniffed in return.

Becca pulled her purse strap over her shoulder and smiled at Heather. "We'll be back in a half hour, tops."

She and Constance argued on the landing and to the steps.

Heather munched a Milky Way Daemon had packed for her and saved the second one for his appointment today. He'd probably be hungry. Keeping him in food was becoming a full-time job.

She checked online coupons and wrote out that day's grocery list. It grew to four pages before she considered what MJ might want to eat. Heather couldn't recall her having had anything last night. Possibly because Daemon had eaten it all.

She'd ask when he came in.

Becca and Constance returned, sipping chocolate malts. Their attitudes toward each other were as frosty as the drinks.

She hoped they hadn't argued about her during lunch. Feeling bad, she had to confess. "It was wonderful."

Constance spun around and raced to her desk. "How wonderful?"

Becca joined them. "You don't have to tell us. What you do on your own time is none of our business."

"I don't mind. It was really wonderful."

Constance nodded. "And?"

Heather couldn't tell them about MJ teaching her to seduce Daemon and to ignore her guilt about that and everything else. Even Constance would be shocked. "Daemon's a good guy. He gave me three Milky Ways."

Constance went blank. She looked at Becca. "What's that code for?"

Becca lifted her shoulders.

They tried to figure it out as they left.

Heather checked the time. Daemon would be there shortly, a polite twenty minutes before his scheduled appointment.

Five minutes later, she hung over the balcony railing and blocked the hazy sun with her hand. He wasn't in the churning crowd below.

The were she'd snapped at the other day saw her and stopped on the steps.

"I'm so glad you're here." Heather crossed to the stairway. "How good are your eyes?"

The color drained from his swarthy face. "Why?"

"I'm looking for someone."

He hurried down several steps.

Heather ran after him. "Not you. Someone on the street. Maybe you can see him better than I can." She described Daemon.

The were gripped the railing, his gaze sweeping tourists, locals and businesspeople. "Nope, I don't see—wait. You said he's missing his feet?"

"No, I said they're beautiful and he should never replace them even though they hurt, which makes him limp."

He shook his head. "Not there. Sorry." He ducked into the building.

Heather followed and escorted him to the treatment room. Back at her desk, she checked the time. Daemon was fifteen minutes late, which meant his appointment was about to begin. She hoped he hadn't passed out from pain or hunger on the way here. He shouldn't have given her the Milky Ways. They might have kept him going.

She wasn't sure whether to run home or call there. Could be he'd simply overslept. Her hands shook so badly, she punched in the wrong number on her office phone.

Once she got it right, she agonized through the first ring and hoped he knew how to answer her smartphone. She'd left it on the kitchen counter but forgot to provide instructions on how to use the stupid thing.

The third ring turned into five then nine. Thankfully, she'd switched off her voicemail.

On the eleventh ring, he picked up. "Uh...yeah...what?"

"Daemon, it's me. Heather."

"Ah, Heather...hey. You're not outside, are you?"

She panicked at his weird question. "What's wrong? Why aren't you here? You have an appointment."

"Where's Daemon?" Becca gestured to the hall. "His treatment room's empty."

"Sorry. I'm talking to him now."

"Everything all right?" Becca's mood grew as somber as her gray silk top and harem pants.

Heather hedged. "I'll rebook him. Sorry." She turned in her chair and kept her voice super low. "Why aren't you here?"

He made a weird noise, halfway between a sigh and a groan. "MJ and I had a fight."

Heather stood so quickly, her thigh hit the desk. "Did you wish for something? *Why*? You know not to do that with her. She's upset about you being her Master. I have to say, I don't blame her. Everyone deserves to be free, especially in this century. Your wish was for food, wasn't it? I should have picked up something for you before I left for work. I'll never forgive myself for —"

"Hold on. It wasn't about food. Although we could use some. Another stack of steaks and prime rib would be nice. A couple of Buschs, too." He spelled the word.

Heather squeezed the receiver. "Why did you two fight?"

"Why else? She didn't obey what I said. And as far as being her Master, it wasn't my choice. I inherited her."

"That's no excuse. What did you tell her to do?" Heather went dizzy. "Did you tell her your feet are ugly? Did she give you different ones?" She pressed her hand to her chest. "Did she put them somewhere they shouldn't be, like on your shoulders? Is that why you couldn't walk here?"

"No, no, no and no. She didn't do anything to me."

Heather sagged against her desk.

"Your apartment, though…"

"What?" She straightened. "Did you tell her to light the candles and she burned the place down? By accident, of course. She wouldn't do that on purpose."

"Oh, really? Since when? But no, she'd didn't burn anything down. Look, I'll try to fix her fuck-up before you get back. No promises, though. If I don't word my wish just right, things could get worse."

Heather couldn't see how. "Leave my place as it is. Don't take any chances."

"But the way I had it was so nice."

His disappointment broke her heart. No way could she tell him how awful it had looked. Of course, MJ's taste could be far worse. Heather dropped to her chair. "Maybe you should put her on. I can talk to her more easily than you can."

"No way. I don't want you asking her to do anything. Promise me you won't."

"Heather." Zoe. She leaned around a jamb. "Got a client here needs healing."

"I'll be right there." She spoke to Daemon. "I have to go. Please hang on and don't wish for anything, including food. I'll bring as much as I can home with me, promise. All your favorites."

"Everything's my favorite."

She already knew that. "What does MJ like to eat?"

"Beats me."

"You've never asked?"

"It never came up."

Possibly because they'd been too busy arguing or having sex. "I'll see you at the usual time."

Heather ended the call, healed the gouges Zoe had put on a shifter's arms then googled what jinns were supposed to eat. A few references claimed they liked bones because they could grow meat on them repeatedly.

She added barbecue ribs to her list.

Daemon stood near the front window of Heather's apartment.

She trudged up the walk.

He reminded himself not to belch or ask for booze and to keep his jeans on until she told him otherwise. Seeing her place as it was now would be hard enough on her. She didn't need him behaving like a beast.

He opened the door before she could get it and took her grocery bags. "Have a good day?"

She squinted at the light behind him and tried to see around his shoulders. "Why is it so bright in there?"

He wished he could keep her from the truth. Unable to, he stepped aside.

Heather's jaw sagged.

His reaction exactly. What MJ had done was pure madness. She'd even told him what each item was so he wouldn't forget.

As if he ever could.

Huge mirrors in ornate silver frames decorated the walls where the red silk panels used to be. Between them, diamond strands twinkled like stars. Two crystal-and-pearl chandeliers rained light over the pale green carpet, snowy cushions and circular bed, its mattress draped in white fur. Feathery plants in ivory pots fluttered in the breeze courtesy of a ceiling fan. It was made from brocaded silk, according to MJ, in an off-white shade and stretched across a mother-of-pearl frame. Another detail from her. Incense burned in two crystal trays. The scent smelled like chocolate. Music pumped from everywhere, a sappy old Carpenters tune that kept repeating.

Daemon shut the door before anyone else saw this travesty. No respectable satyr would ever have a lair like this. He'd busted his ass to give Heather what his gut had told him women wanted and MJ had totally fucked it up.

"I'm sorry." He slumped. "I conked out for a second, woke up and it was like this."

Surprise swept across her face. "MJ acted on her own? Has she ever done that before?"

"Nope."

Heather grew thoughtful. "Did I talk in my sleep last night?"

"Not that I'm aware of. I better put this stuff away." He limped into the kitchen.

She touched a diamond strand and followed. "Are your feet all right?"

"Getting better by the day." He put the barbecue ribs beneath the sink.

Heather took them out and placed the package on the counter.

Daemon was about to toss the steaks and prime rib in the dishwasher when he remembered yesterday's mistake. He put them in the cabinet.

"Fridge." She pointed.

"On it."

"Where is MJ?"

He lifted his middle finger, showing Heather his ring. "I told her she's not getting out until the end of the next century."

"That's not nice."

He gestured to the living room. "And that is?"

"I don't think she did it to be mean."

"Hey, I know she can't help her shitty taste, but she did it without my permission because she knew it'd bug me. I let her come out to get me a Coors—ah…" He cleared his throat. "That is, a cookie. The Girl Scout kind. Thin mints rule. I was hungry. Anyway, she took so long to get it right, I fell asleep, and well, you know the rest. I told her to put this place back the way I had it, which was perfect, and she actually refused." He threw up his hands. "I didn't think jinns could do that. I hollered. So did she. Have you ever heard of anything like that? What kind of a Master would I be if I let it stand?"

"You could try being her friend."

He laughed. "Yeah, right, good one. Wait." Heather wasn't laughing. "You're serious?"

"Call her out, please."

"No. Why?"

"Because we promised to let her hang out with us."

"Since when? I don't recall that."

"Maybe you were asleep. She did say she'd teach me everything I don't know. That's still a lot." She blushed. "We can't go back on our word, or at least I can't. It wouldn't be right."

Daemon rubbed his temple. Didn't do shit to ease his throbbing headache.

"Please?" Heather sagged against him and stroked his pecs.

His muscles danced in response. He caved faster than a sand castle in a hurricane. "Don't wish for anything. Don't even ask for anything, please."

She touched his temple. Like magic, his head felt fine.

"I won't do, either, I promise." She kissed his cheek. "I just want to talk to her."

"Good luck with that. Hang on."

"Wait. Let me do it. She might be easier to approach if I call her out."

Daemon didn't see how unless they shot MJ full of tranquilizers like he'd seen on a TV program about lions. "Be careful."

"I will." She ran her finger around the stone three times in rapid succession.

"Hey." She was doing it wrong. "Not so quick."

Light flashed. Oily black smoke, rather than MJ's usual orange and red, announced her arrival.

She leaned against the opposite counter, arms crossed over her chest, bottom lip thrust out in an obviously crappy mood.

Heather hurried to her.

"Whoa." Daemon grabbed Heather's arm and pulled her back. "Keep your distance. Better still, stand behind me."

She patted his hand, pulled free and rushed to MJ. "It's beautiful. Absolutely gorgeous. You're a genius."

"Oh, yeah?" MJ smiled a little.

Daemon frowned. "You've got to be kidding. No, wait, you're lying to make her feel better."

Heather looked over. "Sorry, no. I can't lie, remember? But I really appreciate what you did when you changed my place, because it came from your heart." She blew him a kiss and cradled MJ's face. "You did this for me, didn't you?"

She shrugged. "Maybe."

"Did I talk in my sleep about it?"

"Nope. It just seemed like you."

"Thanks." Heather hugged her.

Daemon limped across the room and slapped MJ's hand away from Heather's waist. "You actually like what she did better than how I decorated your place?"

Heather ran her forefinger over his bottom lip.

His teeth tingled.

"I'm sorry, but I do. But only because what she did is so gorgeous."

That was supposed to make him feel better? "You're saying mine wasn't?"

MJ smirked. "Not unless gross is the new pretty."

"Hey." Heather pointed. "Be nice. Daemon wants to be your friend, too."

He backed away so fast his ass and shoulder hit the fridge. "I want her to behave. I'm not asking for the moon here."

"That's not true." Heather squeezed his arm. "That's exactly what you're asking for."

Daemon pulled away from her. "Whose side are you on?"

"Yours and hers. You want her to be nice. Maybe she would be if you wouldn't keep her cooped up like you and her other Masters have. She wants to be free, no different from the rest of us. Is that so bad?"

Until now, Daemon had no idea a good fairy could lose her mind. "You do recall what I told you about her separating my legs from my body and my buddy having to run them down."

Heather shot MJ a look. "That was mean."

She stopped snickering. "He was being a prick."

"That word isn't nice, either."

MJ curled her upper lip.

Heather traced it with her fingers and coaxed it back to its usual shape. "I know you can do better."

MJ caved just as Daemon had. "Fine. Is this our first fight? Yours and mine. Can we hug again and make up?"

"Sure."

"Great. I'm glad you like what I did with your place." She grabbed Heather around her middle and swung her off her feet. The bells on MJ's slave bracelets tinkled.

Daemon growled. "Stop it."

MJ released Heather. She staggered back. MJ gave him an innocent look. "Why? Because you want everything to always be about you?"

He slung his arm around Heather's shoulders and pulled her into him. "See what I have to put up with when it comes to her?"

MJ bared her teeth and slipped her arm through Heather's.

Daemon tightened his hold.

Heather shook her head, pushed away from them both and kept her distance. "Come on, the three of us are going to have a nice dinner together. No arguments from either of you."

* * * *

If this didn't beat all. Daemon sat across from MJ at the kitchen table. Heather was at the end, between them, though slightly closer to MJ than she was to him. Two against one. Worse, two women against a guy.

The odds weren't looking good. The truth was in MJ's smug grin. She'd already commandeered the barbecue ribs for herself.

Heather begged him to understand. "She hasn't had regular meals like you have."

Yeah, yeah, yeah. Couturie wasn't the Ritz-Carlton. Before he'd hooked up with Heather, he'd subsisted on grass, berries, occasional wildlife that had dropped dead, whatever the hell the tourists and locals left behind and the stuff he got from MJ with her always misinterpreting what he really wanted. Hardly five-star fare.

He gobbled his steak, prime rib and hot wings quickly and petulantly.

Heather touched his hand.

Daemon spoke with a full mouth. "I'm not going to belch, all right?"

"Thank you." She stroked his fingers. "I missed you today."

He swallowed his barely chewed food and licked her thumb. "I missed you, too. I wore my jeans just in case the pizza guy came over."

"You're a good man."

Not that good. He played with her boob.

Her head sagged to the side.

Just as he liked. "You were gone so long we'll have to make up for lost time tonight."

"Count me in." MJ grabbed the potato salad. "Just like you promised, so I'd get rid of that nasty guilt."

He ignored her.

Heather straightened. "About that."

Daemon didn't want to ask but had to. "You feeling bad again about you and me doing stuff?"

She shook her head.

"Awesome." He dipped his fingers to her crotch.

MJ kicked him.

"Hey." He shot her a murderous look.

She smiled sweetly. "Sorry. Wait, no I'm not. You can thank me for what you're doing with Heather."

"How's that? It's my hand on her, not yours."

She licked barbecue sauce from her lips. "She hasn't run away shrieking. Right, Precious?"

Even the part in Heather's hair got red. "I'd never do that, thanks to both of you. But there is something I need to tell you guys."

The food lay like a brick in Daemon's belly. He brought back his hand.

MJ lowered her rib to the plate. "You're throwing us out?"

"How is that possible?" Daemon tapped his ring. "You live in here. You'll always have a place to stay, even if it's a crappy little cell. Now me?" He didn't want to ask but had no other choice. "Babe, are you throwing me out?"

"No, no." She grabbed his hand. "I've loved what we've done together."

That sounded horrible. She'd used *loved* rather than love. Like what they'd enjoyed was in the past, over and done with. He steeled himself for her next words. That she liked MJ's fashion sense better than his and her companionship too, them sharing girly things rather than having wild monkey sex with him.

He had to face facts. Ugly would never be the new pretty. Heather would keep him around only because she pitied his hideous feet. He'd ditched perfectly good hooves for this—watching her and MJ sharing conversation, laughs and hugs while he could only yearn. "But?" He waited for the other foot to fall, as the old saying went. "There's always a but."

"Actually, there's an and." She beamed at him and MJ. "I want more. All that you guys can teach me and then some."

Daemon exchanged a glance with MJ. She looked as stunned as he felt. "You mean...wait, what do you mean?"

Heather cleared her throat and struggled to speak. Nothing came out.

MJ leaned closer. So did Daemon.

Heather took a deep breath. "K-k-k-kink."

Chapter Nine

Even though Heather hadn't been able to spit out the word like Daemon and MJ would have, that didn't mean she wasn't ready to go to the next level.

No matter how indecent the act, Daemon would never hurt her. Nor would MJ. They both cared. She'd known that for certain when Daemon gave her the three Milky Ways despite his constant hunger, and when MJ had turned this place into a good fairy's version of Heaven.

Their tender concern would allow her to be fully free. To explore where life might take her, just as Becca, Constance and Zoe's friendship had given her enough confidence to run the front office.

Heather had come a long way since she'd been a homeless, unwanted fairy, and she wasn't about to turn back now.

Daemon gawked then regarded her skeptically. Like he didn't believe her transformation was real.

MJ beamed. Barbecue sauce smudged her mouth and chin, her table manners as bad as his. "Way to go, Precious. You know what this means, right?"

Her and them prancing around here naked when they shouldn't be, watching R-rated movies, giving each other massages, Heather taking a sick day, even when she wasn't ill so they could boogie without interruption like last night. She nodded.

Daemon spoke to MJ. "Maybe we should explain to her what kink is."

"You think?"

"Yep."

They talked at the same time. "Bondage, dominance, submission, punishment, a three-way or more, voyeurism, hot damn." Laughing, they leaned across the table and gave each other a high-five.

As friends would do, bonding over what they'd said.

Their words danced like goblins in Heather's thoughts. "What?"

MJ wagged her half-eaten rib at him. Her bells tinkled wildly. "When was the last time we were at Anything Goes?"

"Ages, and that's too fucking long." Daemon shoved half his steak into his mouth and talked around the meat. "I still have dreams about our last night there."

"No shit? Me, too."

Heather gripped the table. "What?"

Daemon swallowed his food and dragged his finger across MJ's plate, scooping up barbeque sauce.

She didn't protest or stab him with her fork.

He sucked the sauce from his finger. "I wonder if Xanthus is still there."

"Oh, my God, what a bad boy." MJ's breasts jiggled with her laughter. "Do you remember what he, you and I did the last time we were there?"

Heather stood so fast she bumped the table. Plates rattled. "What are you guys talking about?"

They looked at her patiently and with sympathy.

Daemon scratched his groin. "Kink."

MJ nodded. "Bondage and dominance and—"

"I heard you the first time." Heather wished she hadn't or had googled the term first before opening her big mouth. She sank to her chair. "You two like stuff like that?"

"Wicked fun." MJ winked at Daemon.

He snickered.

Heather clenched her jaw.

Daemon sobered, patted her hand and wiggled his eyebrows at MJ. "I heard they've cut prices for the ladies on Wednesday nights."

"Yeah? Probably to compete with those new places that opened up."

Daemon scratched his underarm. "Rumor says it's because there aren't enough women to go around. The guys are getting tired of sharing."

"Understandable, though it is a treat for us girls."

They cackled.

Heather buried her face in her hands. Never had she felt as foolish. She'd thought she was on the road to total freedom and pure corruption, yet here she was an outsider again.

Daemon rubbed her back. "You okay?"

"No." She looked up and got ballsy. "I want in. Take me to Everything Goes."

"It's Anything Goes." MJ stroked Heather's arm. "Everything Goes is a second-tier club, not nearly as cool as—"

"Whatever." Heather spoke to Daemon. "I want you to take me there."

"No, you don't."

"He's right, Precious. It's not like we could call nine-one-one if you freak out or faint or—"

"Tell everyone not to belch." Daemon made a face. "Talk like that could start a riot."

"Reprimands are a definite no-no. Guys like to be themselves." MJ inclined her head to Daemon.

He licked barbecue sauce off her plate and the table.

His behavior was impolite but wouldn't deter Heather. "I'll adapt."

She craved that more than ever and not only because she wanted to be guilt-and-doubt free. For a split second tonight, she'd felt like the center of their worlds and needed them to act that way again. Daemon as her one true love. MJ as her BFF, as close to a sister as Heather would ever get. She was being selfish but couldn't help herself. "We can go tonight."

Daemon stifled his belch. His cheeks puffed out. "Nope, we can't. You're nowhere near prepared."

MJ nodded. "Physically or mentally."

Heather's cheese pizza threatened to come up. She swallowed hard. "Meaning?"

"Your clothes for one." Daemon gestured to them. "You've got on so many, not to mention they're all white. The ladies always wear..." His face went slack. He turned to MJ. "What are those things called?"

"Corsets, bustiers, waist cinchers, fetish shoes, masks, harnesses and slave collars generally in black leather." She licked sauce off her fingertips. "Want me to go on?"

Heather didn't but lacked the courage to say so. "After I'm wearing those things, what then?"

Daemon grinned. "You do everything I say."

"He likes to play the big, bad Dom." Delight brightened MJ's gorgeous features. "It's epic, especially with everyone watching and cheering him on."

Heather went cold and hot. Her fear and excitement battled for supremacy. "What's a Dom?"

"The guy who dominates you."

"No one minds their own business while he and the girl do this stuff?"

"The girl is called a sub, for submissive, and she is their business." Daemon devoured the remaining coleslaw. "Exhibitionism is part of the experience."

The room spun. "Okay."

"No, it's not." He gave her a disapproving look just as Becca, Constance and Zoe always did. "Not part of your nature, babe."

Of course it wasn't, but Heather hoped to evolve. "The other day you said you'd like to try everything with me. You've changed your mind?"

"Well, no, but…"

"Prepare me. If you won't, MJ will. Won't you?"

"If she does, it's solitary for the next century or two." He tapped his ring. "No cable, either."

MJ swore beneath her breath.

"Fine." Heather stood. "I should have googled k-k-k… The things you guys gushed about before I said anything so I'd know what's involved. I'll do that now." She grabbed her smartphone.

Daemon cuffed her wrist. "Babe." He stroked her thumb. "You don't know what you're in for."

"Because you won't show me."

He huffed and released her hand. "You win. Take off your clothes. Now."

"What?"

"Strip for us. MJ, move the plates aside."

For once, she did exactly as he asked. Her eyes glittered with enthusiasm.

Daemon stood and pushed his face into Heather's. "You're still dressed. I don't like that." With stunning swiftness, he turned her around and swatted her butt. "Strip right now. Real slow or else." He released her.

MJ sat cross-legged on the table, her chin cupped in her hands.

For the nth time, Karen Carpenter warbled about reaching new horizons in her song *We've Only Just Begun*.

The moment was so unreal, Heather couldn't move.

Daemon snapped his fingers at MJ. "Where's the belt we use for punishment? Don't make me wish for it."

"Never, Master." After a faint pop sounded, a cowboy belt dangled from his hand. Silver studs decorated the tooled black leather. The ends swayed hypnotically, menacingly.

This was totally wrong and unbelievably hot.

Daemon pinned Heather with his gaze. "You've been naughty."

"Better ditch the duds, Precious."

She fumbled with her buttons. Her hands trembled so badly she couldn't get the dumb things to cooperate. Frustrated, she ripped her blouse open. Pearl buttons flew everywhere. One bounced on the table.

MJ caught it.

Daemon slapped the belt against his palm. "Not so fast. Slow down."

Heather's breath came in spurts, matching her thumping pulse. She eased the blouse off her arms an inch at a time and paused frequently to fight her light-headedness.

"Not that slow." MJ drummed her fingers. "We'll be here all night."

Daemon slapped-slapped-slapped the belt against his hand.

Heather's blouse slid past her hands and floated to the floor.

Karen belted her guts out.

Trembling from disquiet and anticipation, Heather sucked in a deep breath, undid her bra clasp and removed the garment.

Daemon propped one foot on his chair. The bulge behind his fly was monstrous. "Such pretty tits."

MJ made a smoky sound well past arousal. "I bet they're tasty, too."

"Look how long the tips are." He rested his forearm on his thigh. The belt tapped his calf gently. "Just right for nipple rings."

"With chains to lead her around." MJ rocked merrily. "Display her to the other men."

"Not for them to touch." Daemon's mood grew dark and possessive. "My cock's the only one she's going to know. I'm her Dom, no one else."

Heather locked her knees to keep from falling.

He looked down his nose at her. "Lose the skirt and panties."

They fell to Heather's feet.

"Such pale skin." MJ tapped her forefinger against her cheek. "Imagine the lovely marks your belt could leave on her ass."

"Not to mention my mouth on her throat. Ditch the duds. Now."

Heather stepped away from her clothes.

Daemon regarded her intently. "Fold your arms over your head."

She gripped her elbows to keep from shaking.

MJ pushed up and craned her neck. Her attention darted from Heather's boobs to her furry mound. Possibly like the spectators at Everything Goes would do. The room pitched. She struggled to stay on her feet.

"Her curls are as blonde as her hair." Daemon's roguish grin widened. "Nice. But I might want to trim them."

"Or shave them off." MJ pumped her fist. "Bare her completely so everyone can see her cunt, folds and clit whenever you want them to."

Heather whimpered.

"Excellent idea." Daemon spoke to Heather. "On the table."

She walked like a zombie, her legs stiff, her mind whirling. She wasn't certain whether he'd shave her or not and if MJ would help hold her down. The thought alarmed and aroused her.

MJ spoke to Daemon. "Sex or punishment first?"

"I'll cut her some slack tonight."

"Righto, sex it is." She positioned Heather on the table as she had on the bed.

Daemon cracked the belt and pointed.

MJ tossed him the ranch dressing they'd used for their hot wings.

Raw lust tinged with playfulness transformed his sweet satyr features. Now, he was pure Master. He poured the dressing on the curls between Heather's legs then swooped down to her cunt.

MJ held her wrists so she couldn't move.

Like she'd want to… Dynamite heat poured from Daemon's lips. His mouth was ruthless, searching and wanting.

Heather arched her back. Each lick on her folds and clit registered in her pussy and spiraled to her limbs.

MJ tightened her hold.

He ate Heather joyously, leaving his moisture and scent behind, but didn't bring her to climax.

Disappointed, she rammed her feet into the table.

Daemon straightened. "Stop that. MJ, conjure up some rope. Wait — shackles. We'll make sure she can't move."

Heather hadn't any plans to do so while she still required release. "I'll be good."

"You better, Precious. Remember, you have to obey." She squeezed Heather's wrists. "Once you do, watch out."

Daemon tore off his jeans. His shaft sprang out, the head plump with passion and reddened in arousal, his balls tight against his body, needing relief.

He rested his forefinger on her lips. "Not a sound from here on out. No cries, shrieks or wails. Not even when I finally let you come. Every noise you make earns you a lick from the belt, understand?"

She was hopelessly lost. A good fairy's curse when it came to wanton pleasure. "You don't want me to have a good time?"

He struggled not to laugh.

MJ stroked Heather's palms. "Lesson number thirty-one, or maybe thirty-two, I forget. He wants you to fight climax until it nearly kills you. When you do come, keep as quiet as you can to intensify the pleasure.

Unless you want to earn extra punishment. That's cool, too."

She had so much to learn and was eager for her next lesson. "Okay. Let's do it."

Daemon rested her calves on his shoulders, fully exposing her damp pussy.

Sweat broke out on her back and neck.

"Tell me you want this." His baritone was deeper than it had ever been. "Tell me I can do whatever I want and you'll submit."

"Okay."

MJ jiggled her wrists. "Yes, Master."

Heather looked at her. "Shouldn't you be saying that to him?"

She chortled. "You should."

There was too much to remember but Heather was willing. "Yes — wait. Shouldn't it be Yes, Dom?"

"Nope. That's what he's known as. You address him as Master."

"Ah." She grew as submissive as she could. "Yes, Master."

Daemon's grin said he liked the address. He stroked Heather's puffy folds and rubbed her clit.

Delight rushed through her. She lifted her chin to the ceiling.

He stopped. "No sounds. One sigh or word and you not only earn more punishment after we screw, I won't let you come during it."

She tightened her jaw.

"None of that, either."

He was killing her and Heather loved it. As a creature born to control every base emotion, she'd win at this and would keep her tongue, submit fully and wait patiently for her due.

Daemon thumbed her nub.

She sweated badly, ready to beg for release.

MJ smoothed her hair and braided one part.

They were both trying to break her.

Heather dug her nails into her palms.

Daemon released her clit. "MJ."

She muttered beneath her breath but did stop messing with Heather's hair. "What?"

"Look what she's doing with her nails. That's not allowed."

Heather finally understood she couldn't show any response. She relaxed her fingers and lay still, not daring to take more than a shallow breath.

Karen sang longingly and endlessly about new love.

Heather wished Karen would shut the hell up.

Daemon resumed teasing and tormenting Heather's clit.

MJ grabbed her wrists.

Warmth and light, joy and expectation rolled through Heather. Her sheath tightened. A pulse beat deep within. Her pussy grew heavy, limbs weighted.

Perspiration ran down her temple, tickling her cheek.

MJ brushed it away.

Heather gritted her teeth to keep from offering a civilized "thank you". She curled her toes.

Daemon stopped.

He couldn't have seen her feet. They were behind his head. He must have felt her muscles bunching on his shoulders. She relaxed her toes.

Daemon entered her in one powerful thrust, his cock sinking as deep as it could go. Their bodies touched.

She lost what scant breath she had. "Oh, Master."

He laughed then got stern. "One more word and this stops."

Heather doubted that. He sweated as badly as she did. They both wanted him to screw her raw. "Okay."

He rode her like a lusty satyr turned shameless Dom, pumping hard yet also stroking her clit lightly.

A cry gathered in Heather's throat, the sound more powerful than happiness from a thousand good fairies that demanded to be free. Before she could make any noise, MJ pinched her wrists. "Uh-uh. Quiet."

It wasn't easy, but Heather stilled.

Daemon's feverish thrusts tempted and excited as nothing else could.

She pressed her ankles against his neck and pulled him closer. She also patted MJ's hand, thanking her for her lessons.

If he could have crawled inside Heather and become part of her blood, heart and soul, Daemon would have. He was beyond being reasonable about this or even simply horny. Hell, he'd tumbled straight into needing her in his life because she was...

No word he knew could describe Heather adequately. She reminded him of a night of uninterrupted sleep, his belly filled with junk food, a keg of Busch waiting for him, the delight in belching heartily.

Fuck, I love her. There, he'd thought it and the world hadn't screeched to a halt.

MJ scooted over and smacked his hip. "Hey, take it easy."

Heather's boobs practically blurred, they shimmied so much. The table bounced from his ardent thrusts.

"Sorry." He slowed down and gently stroked Heather's clit. "You all right?"

Her eyes were unfocused, her face red, mouth hanging open.

Worry gripped him. "Babe?"

She wailed long and loud.

He hoped he hadn't hurt her. "Heather, are you all right? Talk to me." At other times, she wouldn't shut up. Now, when he needed words, she didn't offer any. "Please."

"I'm great. Wow, did I ever…ah…ever…enjoy myself."

Her pussy pulsed around his cock.

That didn't make him any happier. She was supposed to have waited for him. Bummed, he pumped as though his life depended upon it. His ego certainly did. What the fuck kind of Master was he, anyway? MJ never listened to anything he said and now Heather was calling the shots, too.

No more.

He screwed like the beast he was and resumed stroking her clit.

She gagged. "Wait. I can't stand it. It's too wonderful."

Spoken like a good fairy with masochistic tendencies. He didn't slow down. "I want you to come again."

"I can't."

"Not even with me?" Doms weren't supposed to beg, but he had no choice. "Please try. You left me behind."

She pressed her hand to her throat. "I didn't mean to."

He rubbed her clit faster and harder.

Veins popped out on her temples.

"You okay?"

"Go on." She gripped MJ's hand.

"Ow." MJ struggled to get free. Her bells tinkled noisily.

Heather didn't let go. She wailed, moaned, writhed and dug her ankles into Daemon's neck.

He thrust with overwhelming lust and a feeling more magical than a million sunrises.

They came together. Her shrieks drowned out Karen's words that said she and her guy had just begun.

Gasping, Daemon pushed Heather's legs off his shoulders and sagged to her left side, pulling her with him. MJ had already commandeered the right side and was braiding Heather's hair again. Rather than tell the jinni to get lost, he shared the moment with her because it made his little fairy happy.

Heather ran her fingers through his damp hair and eased the locks off his shoulders. "That was awesome."

Nobody boogied like he did. He flexed his weary cock.

Her cunt wiggled around him. She pressed her cheek to his and pulled back instantly.

Daemon prayed she didn't want to get dressed. "What?"

"You need another shave."

He pulled in more air. "Not from you, please."

She laughed.

The best sound the world offered.

Heather slung her leg over his thigh. "What will you wear?"

"Hmm?" His brain was fuzzy, heart slowing down, sleep edging close.

"To Whatever Goes. What will you wear?"

"Anything." MJ gathered more hair and braided it.

Heather twisted around and looked over. "Then Masters don't wear special clothing like their submissives do?"

MJ tittered. "You called the club Whatever Goes. It's Anything Goes. And at the club, it's Dom, not Master, remember? Lesson number fifty-eight."

"Right. Sorry." Heather ran her fingers lightly down Daemon's chest.

Pleasure rippled through him, similar to countless fireflies flitting through his bloodstream. He grunted his thanks.

"So what will you wear to the club?"

He forced his eyes to open. Her skin was rosy from sex. Her sweet, powdery scent no more than a memory. She smelled musky now. They smelled like each other. "What club?"

MJ giggled. "Hold it. I'll take this question for a hundred, Alex. What is Anything Goes?"

Daemon rubbed his face. "Please don't tell me you still want to go there."

"I do." Heather stroked his jawline. "I like when you pretend to be the Master or Dom or whatever."

MJ chuckled.

Daemon ignored her. "Pretend? Okay, granted, I was easy with you just now by not beating your butt. You're a good fairy, for fuck's sake. Anything Goes can get really rough. The satyrs wouldn't only watch us, they'd egg me on and would make comments about you like MJ and I did earlier."

Heather's color faded. "Will they be mean?" She looked down "Will they say anything nasty about my small breasts?"

He wanted to pull her into his arms and never let go. "If they did, I'd fucking tear them apart."

"Oh, no. I don't want any violence."

"Relax." MJ rested her chin on Heather's shoulder. "No one's going to say anything bad about you. You're one perfect babe."

She blushed. "As long as you guys think so."

"This isn't a good idea." Daemon didn't want other guys ogling her. That was his job. "Everyone will be drinking, belching and swearing. You know how you hate those things. And talk about uncivilized. None of the satyrs will be wearing clothes. Only the nymphs will."

"Along with you." MJ worked Heather's hair into a loose ponytail. "Wait till you see the stuff I have."

She smiled briefly and spoke to Daemon, "I promise I won't say anything about their crude behavior. I'll be good in a bad way." She pressed her mouth to his ear. "As submissive as you like. Please, take me there…and in whatever way you can."

Daemon cursed himself for revealing the lifestyle to her, lighting a fire in Heather that she needed to feed. He figured arguing was futile. She had to see this part of life for herself.

He nodded.

"Thank you." She pecked his lips and glanced over at MJ. "What are you doing with my hair?"

"Something you'll like, I hope."

"If it's a good as what you did to the living room, I'm going to love it."

They hugged.

Daemon pushed off the table and left the kitchen.

Heather and MJ's rapid-fire conversation and giggles followed him down the hall.

Chapter Ten

It wasn't like Heather to ask for a favor or actually two. However, she couldn't let Daemon down. She worried about his reluctance to take her to the club and figured he wasn't only concerned about how she'd act but other stuff, too.

She had to fix it.

To that end, she sat across from Becca at a booth in the McDonald's where they'd first met. The lunch crowd was hungry and happy, everyone gabbing as they enjoyed their meals.

Becca had yet to touch her Quarter Pounder with Cheese, Big Mac or sweet tea. Her cautious mood bordered on distressed. This was the first time Heather had asked Becca to lunch in the four years they'd known each other, saying she wanted to spend some time with her. The truth. Of course, there was a lot beneath her explanation that she hadn't gotten into yet.

She tried to make conversation. "You didn't have to order off the McPick 2 menu. You could have gotten anything you liked. My treat." She struggled to smile.

"This is fine. Are you all right?" Becca searched her face. "I'm not prying, but if you need to talk about anything, I'll listen."

"I know you will. Thanks." Heather cupped her mouth to avoid those passing by from overhearing her. "I really hate to ask and I'll totally understand if you say no. It's selfish of me to even consider this. I've told myself that repeatedly, yet I keep coming back to the same—"

"Sweetie." Becca patted Heather's fingers. "It's all right. What do you want to ask?"

She couldn't. She had to. That reality didn't make her feel any better for letting Becca down. "Can I take a few vacation days? I know I shouldn't. I have no right to leave you or the others with no one to do my job. Who'll help the clients fill out their intake forms, heal them when they need it, see to the accounts and make certain we have enough supplies?" She waved her hands. "I'm sorry. Forget what I said. I couldn't—"

"Heather." Becca caught her waving hand and squeezed her fingers gently. "You've been with us for four years and you've never taken a day off."

"I know. It's so wrong of me to think of myself now."

Becca laughed softly. "Sorry. I'm not making fun. It's just that... You do know you have over eight weeks of vacation time accrued. We've all been wondering when you were going to take even an hour of it."

"You don't mind?"

"Absolutely not. Enjoy yourself. What do you plan to do?"

Heather's blood ran cold.

Becca's caution returned. "Is this about Daemon?"

"And MJ."

"Who?"

Heather covered her face and confessed the whole sordid tale—learning carnal stuff from MJ, losing her guilt, pleasing Daemon and seducing him, too. During her admission, she couldn't keep from smiling.

Becca guzzled half her sweet tea and cleared her throat twice. "You sure you know what you're doing?"

"No, but I want to give it a try. You took a chance on Eric, even though you were scared, and look how great that turned out."

"Hon, our first date was having dinner at his Uncle Desi's restaurant, as you well know, not a…" She glanced over. The booth behind her and those to the side were still empty. Even so, Becca leaned forward and cupped her mouth. "Not a free-for-all at a BDSM club for satyrs with a satyr who looks human but is still part-beast and his unstable jinni."

That did sound bad. Heather forced herself to shrug it off. "Different strokes. And MJ isn't unstable. She's just lonely and wanted out of Daemon's ring. Can you blame her?"

Becca downed her remaining tea. "If this makes you happy, I'm good. But please be careful."

"You don't have to worry. They won't let anything happen to me."

"You really love them, huh?"

"Oh, yeah, totally. Daemon's my guy. We were born for each other. And MJ is like the sister I never had. She's my BFF like you and the ladies at work are."

Becca's features softened. "I'm happy for you. But don't tell Constance or Zoe about the satyr club—they'll worry."

"Plus they'll ask for details or tell me I'm nuts."

"That, too. When are you taking off?"

"Tomorrow. I have to do something first." She chewed her lip before plowing ahead. "I need to ask a favor of you, not as my boss, as a witch."

"Are Daemon's feet still hurting?"

"Just a little. He should be totally fine in a couple of days. This is for me."

Becca pushed back in her seat. "You want me to cast a spell on you?"

"I was thinking of a long-lasting potion, something permanent like what you did for Daemon. I wouldn't expect an employee discount. I'll pay full price. Or…"

Rowdy teenagers clomped toward them.

Heather waited for the boys to pass and settle in a booth yards away. "I could ask your mom. Do you think Rowena would help?"

"Depends. What do you want done?"

Heather tried but couldn't get the words out.

"Aw, sweetie." Becca left her side, hunkered next to Heather and hugged her. "Don't change yourself for Daemon. If he doesn't like you as you are he's not worth it."

Heather made a face. The first time she'd done so with Becca and it felt bad, but Becca couldn't have been more wrong. "He thinks I'm perfect the way I am. MJ does, too, and she's unbelievably gorgeous, which means I'm way less than she is."

"Nonsense. There's nothing wrong with you, so what could you possibly want to change?"

Heather finally got brave and told her.

"Awesome sauce." MJ punctuated her comment with a squeal. "This is beyond sweet."

That's not how Daemon would have described the spanking corset MJ inspected. Constructed from black leather, it laced in the back and had two leather bands to support and separate a woman's naked cheeks. According to the still-broadcasting infomercial, this particular product prepared the submissive for discipline and her Dom mounting her after the punishment.

Heather was going to faint when she saw that, which might be a good thing. Daemon pushed up on the fur-covered bed. Thankfully, MJ had replaced Karen's irritating tune with some classic Anthrax. Its deafening bass vibrated the walls and his belly.

Bobbing his shoulders to the beat, he couldn't ignore the fetish wear MJ had fawned over all day. There were racks filled with waist cinchers. The laces resembled tiny whips. Leather panties crowded each other. None had crotches which gave a Dom easy access to his sub's cunt. Chastity thongs abounded. Those came with chains and padlocks.

That was definitely interesting. He crept closer to them.

"Does this look like Precious or what?" MJ held up a black mask, its leather softened by pretty lace, bows and feathers. In her other hand she dangled a bra, also black leather and lace with half cups to expose a woman's nipples.

Daemon's cock stiffened.

MJ smiled slyly.

He tried to deflate and killed his grin.

She tossed the items on the bed. The bra hit his feet. They were still ugly but didn't hurt any longer.

"What do you think?" She pressed an item against herself that was only leather straps and silver buckles.

"What is it?"

"A harness."

Daemon imagined MJ trussed up in it and hanging from a chandelier. That way he could take off with Heather to a few rowdy bars in the French Quarter for a night filled with normal boogieing and private sex. Damn, he'd wanted to change for the ladies and apparently had, turning into a pussy, totally whipped. *Love does that to you, fool.* "No way is Heather wearing that."

MJ stroked the thing tenderly. "It's for me. And don't you dare say I can't go. Heather wouldn't like that."

Tell him something he didn't know. Daemon pushed off the bed and paced, his limp gone. Now, only his shoulders ached from unbearable tension that had built for hours.

MJ tapped her chin. "I just had a thought."

"Hold on to it. You might never get another."

She dropped the harness and fingered the numerous leather straps. Some thick, others thin, each meant to thrill during punishment. "Heather and I might have to go it alone at the club."

Daemon jerked to a stop. He tensed his shoulders. "Not gonna happen even if Heather wants it."

On that, he'd put his foot down.

"No?" MJ regarded him. "How do you plan to get in without a tail, horns and hooves?"

He figured the usual way, a freaking bribe. The satyr community was as bad as human politicians and banksters. Everyone had their hand out. It was the only way to get good stuff like junk food and hard liquor, because those things sure as hell didn't grow in the forest. "We're going to need more cash."

"We?" MJ chuckled. "Given the lack of females, they'll probably let Heather and me in without a cover charge." She lifted her shoulders in a gentle shrug. "Once we're inside, I'm sure some lonely satyr will be happy to buy us a drink."

Daemon growled. "Make that a fucking lot more cash." He'd have to pay the guys to stay away from Heather. As far as MJ was concerned, he hoped one would kidnap her and never send a ransom note. "Don't make me wish for it. If you do, I swear it's in the stone for you for eternity no matter what Heather says."

The music paused between sets. A key sounded in the front lock. Heather back from work.

Daemon reached the door before MJ could. "Hey." He grinned at Heather and the bags she clutched to her chest. "Bet that's dinner. Let me help."

She didn't release the bags.

Daemon tugged harder.

She fought him.

He prayed she wasn't fed up because he'd eaten all her previous stuff and wanted to keep tonight's food for herself. Lifting his hands in surrender, he backed away.

Heather stepped inside and stopped dead. The music was blasting away again, the bass so loud the black leather outfits and chains wiggled.

A pop sounded…MJ doing her magic. Anthrax cut off. Karen returned and trilled away.

Daemon and Heather groaned.

A new pop burst out and the music shut off altogether. MJ padded closer, her bells tinkling with each step. "What's wrong, Precious? Come on, give the bags to me."

Heather clutched them tighter. The paper crinkled.

MJ tried to peer around them. "What are you hiding?"

Daemon leaned down to MJ's ear. "Her food. She doesn't want us taking it anymore."

MJ waved him away and gave Heather a gentle smile. "It's okay. Show us. We won't judge."

Heather blushed vividly and dropped the bags.

A ketchup bottle rolled out. Daemon grabbed it, looked up and gaped.

"Whoa." MJ stared at Heather's breasts. "C's?"

She nodded. "They're too big, aren't they?"

"Not in my world." MJ hurried from side to side, taking those babies in.

Daemon yanked her away. Before she could regain her balance, he clasped Heather's boobs. "What did you do?"

"Changed like you did." She gestured to his legs and feet. Her eyes widened. "You're not limping any longer."

"Feet don't hurt." He thumbed her nipples. They felt so sweet, he wanted to growl like the savage satyr he was. "Why'd you do this to yourself?"

She stepped back and crossed her arms. That deepened her cleavage.

Daemon went from flaccid to rock hard in two seconds flat.

Heather regarded his erection. "So you do like them."

"Well, yeah, but you didn't have to change for me."

"I did it for myself. I want to look hot for the club."

That again. "Heather, babe." Daemon fondled her boobs and nearly shot his wad at how nice they felt. So heavy, warm and soft his balls twitched. "You'd have to wear panties without a crotch or a spanking corset, maybe even a chastity thong." He pressed his cheek to hers "The thong is really cool, by the way." He eased back. "That's not you."

MJ joined them. "Do you like your new boobs?"

Heather smiled shyly. "Yeah. I was just worried how you guys would react."

"What do you think about this?" MJ held up the frothy leather mask.

"Wow. That's so pretty." Heather followed MJ to the racks and combed through stuff. Every move made her new boobs jiggle. She searched the fetish wear intently rather than with horror.

He'd ruined his sweet little fairy.

Heather stroked the same harness MJ had shown him earlier. "How's this thing work?"

"Crisscrosses over your boobs and pussy." MJ held the thing up to herself. "I'm gonna wear it. What do you think?"

"Suits you. You'll look beautiful."

"I thought I'd wear black lipstick, too."

"Good idea." Heather smoothed MJ's tresses. "What are you going to do with your hair? Not that it isn't gorgeous now, but are you going to put it up, tie it back or do something else?"

Daemon resisted the urge to scream.

As the two women gabbed about hairstyles, makeup and other female crap, he put away the groceries and microwaved the ice cream when he shouldn't have. Clearly, the dumb microwave wasn't working. It made everything mushy. After he drank the soupy mess, he pondered how to cook the steaks, not recalling what Heather had done.

He eyed the toaster she always used to make his Eggos. They'd turned out hot and crisp. It should do the same for his steaks. He stuffed meat into the first slot.

"No, wait!"

Daemon looked over. Heather wore the chastity thong, a leather slave bracelet on each wrist and nothing else. Her hair flowed over her chest but her nipples still peeked through.

He tossed the second steak on the counter and hurried to her.

She smiled. "If you wait a few minutes, I'll make dinner."

"Can't. I want to eat now." He hauled her to the bed. She squealed.

Daemon tore off her chastity thong with his teeth, settled between her legs and tasted what he wanted most.

Her heat and musky scent filled him.

* * * *

During dinner, Heather tried not to glance at the fetish wear in the living room but couldn't help herself.

MJ leaned close. "Ready for me to do your makeup and hair?"

She was. Couldn't wait in fact. "Absolutely. We can do it in here. The bathroom's kind of small."

Daemon made a pissed noise. "I. Am. Still. Eating."

He'd chewed his food tonight rather than swallowing it whole as he usually did. The bites he took were so tiny his steaks and pizza still covered his plate.

MJ shrugged. "You don't have to go if you don't want."

"I wasn't planning to." He hunched over his food. "I'm not moving till I'm done."

"I meant to Anything Goes."

"What?" Heather grasped his wrist. Steak fell from his fork to his pec. "You have to go tonight. I took several days off from work so we could stay as long as we wanted. Why wouldn't you go?"

He peeled the meat off his chest and popped it into his mouth. "Not enough cash." He shot MJ a hard stare that said he wasn't going to wish for it. "I have to bribe the bouncers to get in since I no longer have a tail, hooves and horns."

MJ nodded. "The way he looks now, he's pretty much dog meat."

Heather cradled his cheek. "Can't you wear your cowboy hat, jeans and boots to hide what you've become, like when you first came to the service?"

"I wish." He pointed his knife at MJ. "I'm speaking metaphorically, not literally."

She lifted her hands. "I'm not going to do a thing to you unless Precious lets me." She turned to Heather. "How about it? Can I play a little?"

"No. This is serious." She spoke to Daemon. "What did you mean by what you said?"

"Clothes aren't optional for the guys like fetish wear is for you, MJ and the nymphs. It's either a bribe for me or..."

MJ helped him out. "He could ask me to grant a wish for his old self to come back. Just for tonight."

"*No.*" Heather and Daemon spoke as one.

He kissed Heather deep and long. She guessed because she'd sided with him and he liked sex even more than eating.

MJ slung her arm over her chair. "Suit yourselves. I'm only trying to help."

"I know." Heather drew in her shoulders. "How much cash?"

Daemon told her.

She gasped. "I'd have to take out a loan for that."

"I have a better idea." He glared at MJ. "You can go by yourself while Heather and I stay here."

"And waste her new boobs?" MJ grinned mischievously at Heather. "Don't you want to show those babies off?"

Her face got hot. "Actually, I do. I probably should be ashamed of myself for feeling that way."

"Say what?" MJ made a cross with her fingers like people did when they wanted to ward off vampires. "No regrets. Tell me you want to go and mean it."

That wouldn't be easy, but it was time to be bold. She pulled back her shoulders. "I absolutely do, but not without Daemon. You could help him with the cash like you did before, right?"

"Oh, God, no." He moaned. "Not like before. That was a fucking nightmare."

Heather patted his hand. "How about better than before?" She spoke to MJ. "Not stealing, mind you, but if someone lost a dollar bill or two and didn't notice and didn't need it then you could give it to — "

A pop filled the room. Dollar bills covered the table and reached the ceiling. None were mixed with debris or junk like the ones Daemon had talked about before.

"Wow." Heather circled the bounty. The table creaked beneath the weight. "Can you maybe change the one-dollar bills to hundred-dollar denominations?"

"For you, easy-peasy." In a flash, neat cash piles stood against the walls.

Daemon lifted his middle finger and spoke to Heather. "Maybe you should have the ring."

"Oh, no." She squeezed his hand gently. "No one should have it. You should free MJ."

MJ's eyes widened in expectation and what looked like hope.

Daemon looked from Heather to her without comment. He concentrated on his meal, eating as fast as he could, telling them without words that he'd made his decision.

Heather figured he simply didn't trust MJ. She'd screwed with his head too many times, but only because it was her sole means to defy him. It wasn't as though her begging "free me, pretty please" would have worked with him or her other Masters. Faced with that, she'd been unreasonable and hadn't cared, figuring she had nothing to lose. Heather pressed close and spoke softly. "I tried. I'm sorry."

"No biggie." MJ shook off her disappointment. "Let's get you ready. You're going to blow everyone away."

Chapter Eleven

Holed up in the bathroom, Daemon took his time shaving while the girls got ready for that night.

They giggled hysterically.

He shook his head.

He wasn't a bad guy. Hell, he'd put up with more shit from MJ than most Masters would have and had never come close to strangling her. He'd repeatedly caved to whatever Heather wanted and mostly enjoyed letting her lead him down the wrong paths.

Not this time.

Freeing MJ was too scary to contemplate. Bringing Heather to Anything Goes could signal the end of their budding relationship.

His chest and gut ached.

She'd probably end up liking another satyr she'd meet tonight. Possibly dozens would catch her eye. Could be she'd find their hooves sexier than his ugly feet. Daemon hung his head. Becca had warned him to be careful what he asked for. He hadn't listened to her or to Heather when she kept telling him not to change.

Too late for him to heed that advice now. Heather, too. She'd been as headstrong as he was and had new boobs to show off to every fucking guy at the club this evening and those she'd visit in the future.

He'd turned his precious fairy into a party animal. He wanted to shriek. No way could a satyr break down and cry.

Clicking sounded in the hall. Those footfalls grew closer.

If Daemon had to guess, he'd say those sounds came from high heels. MJ had already worked her magic on Heather.

The clicks stopped outside the bathroom door.

He didn't want to look, but had to.

Heather's hair cascaded in alabaster waves and surrounded her gorgeous face. She wore the pretty mask. Its feathers trailed down her downy cheeks and pointed to her plush mouth glossy with black lipstick.

He dropped the razor and clutched the sink to remain on his feet.

Gold rings adorned the long tips on her tightened nipples so her Dom could slip a chain inside those hoops and use it to lead her around. She'd worn the half-cup bra and crotchless thong, her pale curls trimmed to reveal her puffy folds, her cunt's readiness for a man's cock.

Womanly moisture glistened on those lips.

The room lurched. Daemon locked his knees to steady himself.

Slave bracelets and thigh-high boots with six-inch heels completed her outfit.

His rod got hard so quickly it just about jerked him toward her. Her fragrance wafted close, the scent no longer innocent and powdery but rich, dark and provocative.

A pink flush tinted her cheeks. "Is it all right?"

It was pure wrong for a good fairy but fan-fucking-tastic, too. Daemon wanted to answer her but couldn't get his voice to work.

"It's awesome." MJ joined them. She wore a lacy black facemask and the leather harness, which showed off her shaved pussy. Excitement flared in her violet eyes. "Time to boogie."

She laced her fingers with Heather's and stepped back.

Daemon gripped MJ's other hand and held tight, afraid she'd leave him behind. "Where's the cash for me to buy my way in?"

"The kitchen where it's always been. Go on and get it then finish shaving. We'll wait."

The moment he turned his back on her, she'd whisk Heather away.

"I'll go." Heather stroked his pecs. "You can finish up." She hurried down the hall, wobbling badly on her spike heels. Her adorable ass bounced with each tentative step.

Absolute wonder filled Daemon.

MJ tapped her foot.

Her presence killed the magic. "You know I can't trust you, right?"

"You never gave me a chance."

He tramped to the sink and eased the razor over his throat, the last part he needed to shave. "You fucking turned my life inside out."

"And mine was a trip to Magic Mountain?"

"I wasn't the one who put you in the damn ring in the first place."

Grunting and scraping noises sounded in the hall.

He finished shaving quickly, wiped his face off and left the bath.

Heather dragged two large bags toward him.

Daemon rushed to her. "Let me help."

Once he had the money pressed to his chest, he snatched MJ's hand and forced himself to forget their previous animosity. "Do your thing." He squeezed her fingers lightly. "Please."

Heather smiled at his wimpy request.

MJ vacillated between surprise and wariness. "Yeah, sure. Hang on."

Heather scarcely had a chance to heed MJ's suggestion. The jinni whisked them from the apartment hall to a forest. They faced a sheer rock wall with a domed entrance. Something Heather had never seen in New Orleans. "Is this Couturie?"

"Quite a bit north." MJ pulled her into the cave.

Clammy air brushed past Heather, the rock walls so close she drew in her arms and gripped Daemon's hand.

"It's okay." He caressed her fingers. "I won't let anything bad happen to you, ever."

Heather halted at that word *ever*. She pulled away from MJ, threw her arms around Daemon and hugged him as hard as she could. "I know."

Happy tears stung her eyes, her love for him bubbling over. She kissed his ear and cheek and rubbed hers against his freshly shaved skin.

He dropped the money bags. With his hands on her ass, Daemon pushed her into his cock, his rod hard as steel, smooth as silk, hot as a New Orleans summer. He captured her mouth, plunged his tongue inside and took what was his.

Heather sagged into him. Their legs bumped.

A low, steady throb rumbled close, sounding like a monster's heartbeat.

"Oh, my God. Slayer." MJ boogied hard. "Hot damn. Come on."

Daemon released Heather and scooped up the bags. He tugged her through the darkness and followed MJ.

Heather held back. "What's Slayer?"

"The music. Fucking awesome." His shoulders bobbed to the rough beat.

Ahead, torches ate away the darkness. The light spilled over a brawny satyr sporting impressive horns and a long tail. Arms crossed over his chest, he leaned against the rock wall, ready to nod off, despite the thunderous bass.

MJ cooed loudly. "Hey, baby."

He turned his face to her. His limp cock hardened instantly, ready for some serious action. His wide grin grew hungry. "Hey, there."

In a flash, MJ was on him, kissing him hard, grinding her mound against his cock, touching him everywhere.

Heather supposed they knew each other. Maybe he'd been an earlier Master and she was glad to see him again, even though he'd previously been a louse.

After numerous grunts and groans, she stepped away and readjusted her harness. "Whew, I needed that."

"I did, too." He smoothed his hair. "What's your name?"

"Whatever you want it to be."

He looked fascinated. His gaze drifted to Heather. He actually drooled.

Rather than shrink back, she forced herself to be confident and bold.

Daemon swore softly and pulled her behind him.

The satyr glared at Daemon's feet.

Heather broke free and tottered toward the guy as best she could. The heels were killing her. "His feet are beautiful."

It mystified her why no one else thought so.

The satyr leered at her nipple rings and crotchless thong.

She'd felt naked before. Now even her face mask didn't offer protection.

Oddly enough, curiosity and lust burned beneath her hesitation, encouraging her to have the best night of her life so she could laugh and reminiscence about it as Daemon and MJ had with theirs.

Daemon shoved the bags into the satyr's chest. "Cover charge. Enjoy." He patted the guy's cheek.

"Daemon?"

"Yep."

"Hey, it's me, Faustaff. Been a while since we rapped. What the fuck happened, man? Who did that shit to you?"

Heather huddled closer to Daemon. "I like his feet."

Faustaff lifted his bushy eyebrows. He elbowed Daemon. "Good luck in there. New crowd. No one you know."

Heather hugged Daemon's arm. "I won't let anything bad happen to you."

"I take it she's never been here, right?" Chuckling, Faustaff gave Daemon a thumbs-up.

Heather's resolve wavered, but only slightly. To turn back now would mean never experiencing this…whatever it might be.

Inside the club, more torches burned, giving the place a cozy yet lewd feel. Smoke and sexual odors permeated the place. Satyrs lounged on black or red pillows. Some held beer bottles, others mixed drinks. Nymphs knelt in front of them in submissive poses or were chained to the rock walls. Each female had dressed in her tawdry finest, the corsets, bustiers and cinchers in black leather. None hid the ladies' mounds or breasts. The guys were comfortably nude, tails swishing, hands roaming, mouths and bodies joined to their babes, taking what they willed.

What Heather suspected the nymphs wanted. Their eyes were beyond glazed, their smiles delirious. *Interesting.* And arousing.

MJ danced to the beat, arms above her head, hips gyrating. "Oh, yeah."

Daemon did a bump and grind around MJ, tapping her hips and ass with his.

A loud wail cut through the noise.

Heather flinched and looked over.

A nymph clad in nothing except slave bracelets had her arms above her head, wrists attached to a post, ass facing an audience filled with satyrs.

They stomped their hooves. "Again."

They'd shouted together.

The pleasingly plump and lovely nymph wiggled her booty.

A satyr next to her lifted his leather strap and swung it against her butt. The crack echoed through the room and mingled with the music. She cried out, though, not in pain. More like she was enjoying an orgasm.

Heather's pussy pulsed with interest.

"Hey, you!" A satyr across the room pointed at Daemon. "What the fuck?" The guy stomped over.

Daemon stopped dancing and squared his shoulders, ready to rumble.

"No, wait." Heather pushed between them. "No need to fight. I love his feet."

Daemon groaned.

She had to get better at this or she'd get him killed. "Whoa, whoa, whoa." She held out her hands to keep the pissed-off satyr from charging. "We paid. We deserve to be in here."

The satyr glowered. His buddies noticed Daemon and looked murderous.

"This isn't what it seems." Heather had to shout above the music. "He's not mortal. He's a beast like you guys."

She told them how Daemon had come to the service for a makeover. His long trek from Couturie. His bruised hooves and bleeding ankles. His poor ripped-off horns.

"Ah, Precious." MJ slung her around Heather's shoulders. "A little advice. They don't want to hear that, especially Daemon."

Embarrassment darkened his face.

This was all her fault. She'd insisted they come here and now he wasn't only humiliated but might face a brawl that could turn out to be a hundred against one. "We should go."

He growled. "You mean run?"

Heather would have said yes as the obvious answer, but figured that would only infuriate him more. "Whatever happens, I'll heal you."

He trembled with outrage. Veins protruded on his neck and chest. "You think they're gonna beat my ass?"

"No." The truth. "But you might hurt yourself a little bit by beating theirs. I'm here to help."

He shot her his puppy-dog look.

Her heart swelled with boundless love, but she also worried about the coming melee. "MJ." Heather elbowed her and kept her voice low. "Say something to stop them from hurting him."

"Anything for you, Precious." She faced them. "Before you guys tear each other apart, why not let Daemon and Precious do their thing?" She gave Heather a wink. "How's that?"

It wasn't what she had in mind, but anything for her baby... "Ah, yeah. Let us do that. Like I said, we did pay to get in here."

"Big deal." The nearest satyr swaggered closer to her. "Who are you? Or rather *what* are you, Precious?"

"His fairy slave." She smiled proudly.

The satyrs exchanged glances.

MJ clasped Heather's shoulder. "You're his submissive. Drop the fairy stuff. Not cool." She hollered to the guys. "Want a great show or do you want to hear yourselves talk?"

Their grumbles quieted.

The one who'd asked Heather's identity flexed his muscles. "Be our guests. Put on your show. Now."

Daemon grabbed Heather's arm. "You don't have to do this."

"I want to." Not only to spare him a fight, but because she was growing increasingly curious. To have him disciplining her in front of the others and doing whatever else he and she wanted was a sure way to rock her previously dull world and to make her the kind of woman they both deserved. "Take me, use me, punish me." She spoke to MJ. "Make sure he does, please."

MJ grinned.

Daemon's pupils dilated even more.

The satyr tossed him a thin gold chain.

Daemon slipped it through Heather's nipple rings and wrapped the ends around his hand.

The crowd parted and allowed them to pass, barely. The satyrs leaned close, forcing Heather to brush against them. They leered, sniffed and murmured lewd nothings.

Now, she felt unbelievably nude.

Daemon glared at the crowd. His heavy breathing and clenched fists warned them to back off.

They did.

He led Heather to what she guessed was the main performance area, a circle surrounded by cushions and lit with torches. In the center stood a simple frame. Chains hung from the top and bottom beams. Whips, riding crops and straps lay nearby.

She broke out in a sweat. Not entirely from apprehension, but brazen desire she didn't know she owned.

The satyrs led their ladies by chains in their collars or through their nipple rings. The nymphs' fleshy asses bore red marks from their punishments. They knelt at their Doms' hooves or lounged on the cushions and spread their legs.

Heather lurched on her heels.

Daemon brought her to the frame, gave her a quick wink and kissed her savagely as a Dom would.

She clung to him, grateful for his strength since her legs were ready to give out. His kiss corrupted thoroughly, his passion so luscious she loosened her mouth beneath his and sucked his tongue, never wanting this to end.

He pulled away, leaving her bereft, dizzy and weak.

"I'll get these." MJ fingered the chains on the frame.

He tested the whips and straps, flicking each in the air.

MJ giggled excitedly. "Gonna get hot now."

She slipped the chains through the rings on Heather's slave bracelets and around her ankles then secured her to the frame top and bottom, spread-eagle, totally vulnerable.

Moisture seeped from Heather's pussy, drenching it. Air brushed her ass and cleft. Her nipples tightened and her cheeks burned.

"Oops, almost forgot." MJ looped the chain in Heather's nipple rings and secured them to the top of the frame.

A satyr directly in front studied Heather's pussy as he played with his nymph's boobs.

Another satyr licked the nymph's cleft. His grunts and her moans betrayed their delight.

Fighting dizziness, Heather looked over. Daemon had chosen a broad leather strap for discipline. His cock was erect. Pure sin filled his eyes.

"This needs to come off." MJ unhooked the front clasp on Heather's bra. The cups pulled away from her breasts. Her huge mounds fell into MJ's willing palms. She lifted them to the guys. "Are these nice or what?"

They applauded, whistled and stomped.

She spoke to Heather. "Remember, no regrets."

"Never." This was off-the-charts great.

"Good girl." She swatted Heather's ass.

"Fuck, that's nothing." A satyr stomped his foot. "What kind of Dominatrix are you?"

MJ swiveled her hips. "I'm not. I'm a jinni who likes to be told what to do."

"Yeah?" He curled his finger, gesturing her over. "How about making me happy?"

"Is that a wish?"

"*No*." Heather blinked at her shriek. She lowered her voice. "That is, she doesn't do wishes. Do you, MJ?"

"Not if you don't want me to. But I was hoping to have some fun…"

Heather nodded. "As long as it doesn't involve a wish, I'm good with it."

MJ and the guy rolled across the ground, kissing, groping, having a grand time.

Another satyr growled. "When's the damn show gonna start? Pink up her ass. Eight licks."

Another patron shook his fist. "Fuck eight. Ten."

Daemon roared. "My damn choice — no one else's." His voice was deeper and grittier than the rest. All man.

They fell silent. The music pounded and thumped in time with Heather's heart. Her ears buzzed.

Daemon towered over her. "Not one sound." He'd spoken loud enough for everyone to hear. "You whimper, moan or cry out, and you'll get more punishment."

MJ pulled her mouth from the satyr's. "So fucking hot. Go for it, Precious."

Heather would.

The music paused.

Daemon stepped back. His feet slapped hard against the packed dirt floor.

Whistles rippled through the crowd. Satyrs edged closer and stared at her stretched out and displayed.

The closest one made an approving sound. "Nice tits."

She beamed and would have thanked him, but Daemon had ordered her to be quiet.

"I like her ass." This satyr owned more bulk than the others. "I say bend her over and let's play."

Her face got even hotter.

Daemon charged the others. "Quiet."

They fell silent and skittered back. The music roared to life, the bass booming wildly.

She panted, unable to help herself.

Daemon returned and licked her right nipple.

His damp mouth did more than arouse, it calmed. Even in punishment, he'd never hurt her.

He rounded the frame. His shadow slanted across the rock wall. He wrapped the strap around his hand, brought his arm back and lifted it.

The music stopped again.

Something whistled.

The leather struck her with a single sharp crack.

Heather jerked at the sound. The sting registered next. Biting back a startled gasp, she pushed to her toes. Before she was able to catch her breath or sink back down, warmth replaced the pain and spread through her like liquid sunshine.

MJ was right. Hot. Heather tugged on her restraints and begged. "Again."

The crowd cheered.

Daemon licked her three more times in different spots.

Perspiration ran down her face. Her pussy couldn't get juicier.

He stroked her clit, sucked her nipples and settled his cock in the furrow between her cheeks. He leaned around to capture her mouth and snatched her breath. No words or sounds could escape.

The room dipped, swayed and spun crazily.

Wasn't enough. She wanted more.

He unchained her and positioned Heather on all fours.

With one hand on her belly and the other on her back, Daemon directed Heather to lift her ass to show off each mark from the strap. This wasn't for his gratification, but hers. She craved what they'd done. Delight lingered in her eyes.

His little fairy liked being bad. Surprisingly, she was also an exhibitionist.

"Nice." The satyr who'd spoken belched long and loud.

Daemon ignored the crude bastard and the others. He positioned himself between Heather's legs.

MJ and her satyr friend rolled into the scene. She gave Daemon and Heather a thumbs-up then got back to business with the guy, straddling him. As she took his cock into her cunt, he bellowed loudly and happily.

Mundane stuff. Time for some real action.

Daemon yanked Heather's thong down to fully expose her slippery cleft and entered her in one smooth, prolonged thrust.

She pressed her fingers into the dirt floor and breathed hard.

The response he wanted.

He knew what else he had to have. Her in his life, tonight, tomorrow and his remaining days. Didn't matter if she asked him not to belch, drink or swear, as long as she wanted him that was good enough. Shit, that was heaven.

Her pussy tightened around his needy rod. She wriggled her ass into him, trying to get closer. A gift that made Daemon feel a hundred feet tall, hung better than any satyr past or present and king of the pissing world.

Holding her hip, he pumped slowly and stroked her nub.

She bucked and moaned wantonly.

MJ and her guy made lewd noises.

Daemon couldn't deny how pleased he was. At least with MJ busy, she wouldn't destroy this place or do something to him that Heather would have to fix.

Concentrating on her tight heat and her slippery-smooth cunt, he rode her long and hard. The blaring music and vulgar comments receded. Only she existed.

Her sheath grew narrower, or maybe he got harder and larger, Daemon wasn't sure, but he sensed they couldn't wait any longer.

He increased his pace, thrust more forcefully and teased her nub with quick strokes.

She shrieked and moaned, the noises uninhibited, as free as she'd desired. She climaxed hard.

Satyrs and nymphs cheered.

Daemon worked Heather for the next round and joined in this time, letting loose, shouting louder than the music, beast and man mingled.

For the moment, both were content.

He snoozed without meaning to. When he woke, Heather was watching MJ go at it with another satyr, this one bigger than the last. She rode him as she would a bucking bronco. Her wild cries peaked and died down,

Heather clapped.

Daemon cuffed her wrist.

She leaned into him. "I'm glad she's having a good time. She deserves it."

He guessed. Heather was his only concern. He claimed her mouth then her pussy, lapping her dew and his cum.

Satyrs commented lewdly.

Daemon brushed off their idiotic behavior. He was too intent on tasting, smelling and mounting Heather to do anything else.

He enjoyed her twice more before they fell asleep, snuggled together like spoons.

Two nymphs woke him. He pushed their hands away from his junk. "Don't you have your own guys?"

The red-haired nymph nibbled his shoulder. "We do. They can join us for a fivesome."

In times past, that would have sounded pretty damn nice. Not now. "I'm good." He shook her off.

"How about your fairy slave?" The blonde nymph eyed Heather hungrily. "Think she'd like to play with us and our Doms?"

Not unless it was over his dead body. "How about you girls move on and bug someone else?"

They gave him the finger and padded away.

Thankfully, Heather snoozed through the encounter. Daemon didn't want to give her ideas about having fun with anyone else but him.

Although he would have liked to whiz back to her apartment for some private pleasure, she hadn't asked to leave the club.

They stayed through the night and during the following days.

With each passing minute, Heather became increasingly popular. Other satyrs offered her drinks and a ride on their stiffened rods.

"Come on, Precious." The prick who'd said that stroked his massive cock. "You haven't lived until you've tried me."

Daemon tensed.

Heather gave the satyr a gentle smile. "Thanks, but no. However, I'd love to heal your split hoof. It must really hurt."

He whimpered. "It does. Put your hands on me. All over me."

To Daemon's relief, she restricted herself to the SOB's injury.

"Hey, Precious." Another satyr waved her over. "I have bite marks on my thighs. Don't know how that could have happened."

She gave him a censuring look. "Honestly?"

He lowered his face. "Can you heal them? Please?"

"Of course." She wiggled his way.

Others wanted her gentle attention.

She roamed the club, tending the injured and sick.

Given how much everyone drank, fought and partied, she had her hands full but never complained.

Daemon was proud of her, but scared, too. She'd turned the other satyrs down this time. What about her future visits here?

He'd given her a taste of the forbidden and she liked it a lot, probably too much. He'd been a fool for bringing her here. He knew that now more than ever.

These guys, like him, had fallen hopelessly in love with her.

Chapter Twelve

Switching gears from badass chick to good fairy was murder for Heather.

She should have been careful with what she wished for but couldn't dwell on the problem now. She had to get ready for her first day back at work.

Wasn't easy. Her regular clothes seemed so blah. Too much blinding white. Maybe she'd buy something in tan or oatmeal, mix things up.

Dressed, she made a bowl of Cocoa Puffs for MJ, her fave breakfast, and thirty Eggos for Daemon, drowned in syrup just as he liked. Hopefully, that would make him happy.

He'd been different since they'd gone to the club, the change happening before they'd returned to her apartment. He was quieter now, less playful. Heather wasn't certain why and hesitated to call him on it, afraid his answer might hurt her.

Shortly after they'd left the club, she'd asked MJ about his moodiness. "Is something wrong with Daemon?"

"You're just now noticing? He is who he is. Nothing can be done about it."

Heather had slapped MJ's arm and sucked in a breath at her outrageous behavior "Oh, no, I'm so sorry. Forgive me for doing that."

"You got it." MJ had hugged her hard.

Pleased they were on good terms again but still concerned about Daemon, Heather had broken free. "I meant is Daemon upset about something? He's different than he used to be."

"Maybe he's hungover."

Daemon hadn't had one drink while they'd been at the club, even though his nature was to let loose and have a good time. At first, Heather had thought he'd wanted to stay sober and conscious to serve as her protector. Finally, she'd considered he might be afraid she'd embarrass him again, as she had when they'd first arrived, and had decided to keep a close eye on her mouth. "Maybe I should apologize for mentioning his makeover to the others."

"They'd already noticed. Relax. He's probably just tired from partying. Ignore him."

Heather worried.

Daemon took small bites at breakfast and actually chewed each mouthful three times before swallowing.

Something was seriously wrong.

"Are you feeling all right? Are you getting sick?" She didn't know if satyrs fell ill as mortals did. She felt his forehead. His skin was cool. Heather wasn't certain whether that was okay or not.

Daemon patted her hand. "I'm good."

"You're sure? You're not wolfing down your breakfast."

"Not hungry." He left the table then came back and gathered her in his arms.

She hugged him as hard as he did her and returned his deep, wet, lingering kiss with all the passion and love she owned. When their mouths finally broke free, she clung to him.

Daemon stroked her hair. "Have a good day."

He pecked her nose, regarded her with yearning and returned to bed.

Heather gripped MJ's shoulder. "You take care of him while I'm gone. Don't give him even a moment of grief. If he needs anything or if he is sick, you call me immediately." She put her smartphone next to MJ's place setting. "Understand?"

MJ stopped slurping her cocoa-colored milk. "Yeah, but everything's cool. Relax. You'll give yourself a stroke."

"Call if anything happens." Heather showed her how to use the phone. "Don't forget, please."

* * * *

She arrived at work twenty minutes before schedule so no one would have a reason to stare at or question her.

Becca offered a neutral smile that grew strained. "Morning. Enjoy your days off?"

Heather nodded.

They left it at that.

A short time later, Constance studied Heather's makeup-free face and blouse buttoned to her throat.

Heather couldn't keep still. She knocked over the pencil cup on her desk.

Constance rocked on her heels. "Everything all right?"

"If you mean while I was gone, nothing happened with anyone, especially him."

"Him?"

"You know who I mean. Nothing happened, all right?"

"Yeah, I already figured as much." Constance shook her head and left the reception area.

Zoe was so busy wrestling a were to the treatment table and strapping him down, she didn't notice Heather's return.

Relieved, she dove into today's appointments, fixing what Constance and Zoe had messed up, then she attacked the accounts.

The payables were done when the phone rang. She picked up the receiver. "From Crud to Stud. How can I help—"

"Come home." MJ breathed hard. "*Now.*"

Heather's stomach sank. "What's wrong?"

"Daemon's gone."

"What?" Heather jumped up. "What do you mean he's gone? Where? Did you check the courtyard? Maybe he's out there communing with nature like he did in Couturie."

"He's gone, Precious. He left his ring on the kitchen table."

Heather wanted to be sick. "How is that possible? He said he couldn't take it off. Did you guys fight? Did you say something to him?"

"We didn't talk at all. I was on the bed watching a *WWE RAW* marathon when he suddenly rolled off the mattress, patted my head and went into the bathroom. He came out dressed in his jeans, boots and tee, fooled around in the kitchen for a few seconds then strode to the front door and said, "'Bye. Be good to Heather. Please.' After that, he left."

Heather wanted to throw up. "Can't you materialize to wherever he went, like you did when you took us to the club?"

"He's not my Master any longer. The cord connecting us is broken. I don't know why. Maybe because of you. I'm guessing you're my new Mistress."

"Don't say that. I'd never lock up anybody, especially someone I love like a sister."

MJ drew in a sharp breath.

Heather could barely take in air. Her hurt was too bad. "Do you have any idea where he might have gone?"

"Couturie? Are you going after him? I love you, too, by the way. You're the family I never had."

"I know. Same here. Gotta go. Don't leave my apartment."

"I won't, prom—"

Heather killed the call, knowing it was rude, but she didn't have time for niceties. She bolted down the hall and skidded to a stop at a treatment room.

Zoe was inside, strapping another were to a padded table.

"I need your help." Heather flapped her hands. "Now."

Zoe ran to her immediately and looked past. "One of the zombies bothering you? A demon?"

"What's going on?" Becca hurried down the hall, Constance on her heels.

Heather tried not to cry. "Daemon left. I think he's on his way back to Couturie. He was different after we went to the club. I shouldn't have told everyone I liked his feet. Please." She gripped Zoe's shoulders. "You have to drive me to the forest. I love him. I can't let him leave without telling him that, even if he doesn't love me back."

Zoe looked at Becca.

"Take her there." Becca cradled Heather's face. "Good luck, sweetie."

"Thanks." She wanted to say more to be polite but there wasn't time. She raced to the front door, Zoe close behind.

Constance called out, "Don't let that hottie get away!"

Zoe gunned her hearse down the city streets and took the most direct route to the forest. Luckily, most drivers pulled into other lanes, giving her a clear path.

Could be they thought this was the lead vehicle in a funeral.

Heather rocked in her seat. "Can't you drive faster? Don't you have a siren or something?"

"This isn't an ambulance." Zoe swerved around a truck, made it through a yellow light and pumped her fist.

Clutching the dash, Heather checked the area for Daemon. Only mortals milled about in the mild, sun-drenched day. Maybe they'd seen him and could tell her what direction he'd taken, unless he was on another street entirely. She tried to figure out how far he could have gotten in the time he'd been gone but couldn't.

Not only was she a dummy and a fool, she was a coward, too.

She should have told him how she felt, but no. She'd been too scared, thinking he'd reject her. At least if he had, she would have known for sure where they stood and could have tried to change his mind. This was so much worse. To never see Daemon again or know where he'd gone...

Tears stung her eyes.

Broad shoulders and bronze skin flashed in her peripheral vision.

She sat up. "Stop!"

Zoe hit the brakes. The hearse fishtailed.

Tires squealed and horns blared. The driver behind them leaned out his window and shouted obscenities.

Zoe turned in her seat and bared her teeth at him.

He shut up.

Heather craned her neck. It *was* Daemon's skin and shoulders. She popped her door and pried Zoe's fingers off her arm. "I'm okay. Go on and park. Don't come with me, please."

Heather dashed across the traffic lanes to a grassy spot that faced mom-and-pop businesses.

Bikers rode past, lovers strolled, kids ran rather than walked and tugged on their parent's hands to get them to move faster.

Daemon sat beneath a moss-draped live oak, boots off, his left foot cradled in his palm.

Panting, Heather fell to her knees at his side. "You're hurt. Your feet are bothering you again. It's my fault." She reached for his foot to heal him.

Daemon stared and pulled away. "What are you doing here? Wait." He spoke through his teeth. "Dammit, MJ." He swore beneath his breath.

"You're mad at her for telling me?" Tears ran down Heather's face. "You left. You didn't even say goodbye. You left."

He looked sad and uneasy. "I have to go."

She clasped his wrist to keep him from grabbing his boot. "I've been too demanding, haven't I? What is the matter with me? I never should have asked you to take small bites and chew slowly and not to belch. Or told you to cover yourself in public. I've been relentless. It was too much for you to take. I can't blame you."

"Hold on. Yeah, you've nitpicked every freaking thing, but other than that, you're perfect."

"Not if you're leaving me. I must have done something horribly wrong."

He looked past her.

An elderly couple watched them.

Daemon shot the man and woman a hard frown.

They scurried away.

He pulled Heather's hand off him. "You're not the problem. I am."

"What — why? Do you like one of the nymphs you saw the other night? You're meeting her in Couturie? She has more to give you than I do?"

"No." He reached for his boot.

Heather threw the stupid thing. It landed near a trash receptacle. "You're not leaving until you tell me why. I want the truth."

It would probably kill her, but she had to have it.

"Fine." He mumbled something then sagged. "I don't like other guys thinking they can come on to you when you're supposed to be with me. I don't want to share you. I don't want anyone to see you naked or watch what we do. It's private. It's for you and me." He shrugged. "And maybe MJ if she wants to keep you prisoner so I can do my thing. But not the others. And I don't like your new boobs, either." He gestured to her chest. "They're not you."

Heather had to agree. Carrying around the extra weight was murder. "If I get rid of them, will you come back?"

"I can't."

"Why not? I adore you. Living without you isn't something I can or want to imagine. Can't you ever love me?"

"Can't? Ever? What are you talking about?" His voice trembled. Tears filled his eyes. "I worship you. Fuck, I can't live without you, but I have no other choice."

Heather clutched his hands, unable to let go. "That doesn't make sense. Loving each other is a good thing."

"No." He cleared his throat. "It'd never work out. You have to pay for everything. You're going broke keeping me in food. I contribute shit. I don't have a job, a skill or a future. The only thing I do is lay around all day watching cable and give you epic orgasms when you come back. I'm worthless."

"That's not true." She squeezed his fingers. "You just got your new legs and feet. Give yourself time to find out what you want to do."

"And that would be?"

Heather scoured her mind and came up with zip. "What did you do in the forest?"

"Drank and screwed nymphs."

She clenched her jaw.

"You're about to break my hands, babe."

Heather loosened her grip. "As long as you don't want to do that any longer…"

"You mean cheat on you?" His mood darkened. "Not a chance. Ever. How about you when it comes to me?"

"Are you kidding? I'm offended you'd think such a thing. Just because the other satyrs asked me to ah…to ah…"

"The word is screw."

"Whatever. That didn't mean I was remotely interested. Surely, you must have known as much."

"Like you knew how I felt about MJ when I called her out the first time and she was all over me?"

He had a point. Heather recalled her foolish jealousy. "We can work this out."

"No, we can't, unless you want MJ to keep finding lost money that she and I will contribute to the pot."

"That's no solution." Stuff like that should go to charity, the homeless, women's shelters and school lunches for kids. "I'm not letting you go. We'll get you a job. MJ, too. By the way, thanks for freeing her."

Daemon shrugged. "It was the right thing to do. She'd done her time and I didn't want to take her away from you."

Is any other guy as good? Heather kissed his knuckles. "Would you mind if she's our houseguest? She's never been on her own. I don't want to put her out. I swear, I'll talk to her and she'll behave."

"You don't know MJ."

"We'll work it out. I want to give her a place where she feels at home until she finds her own guy."

"Seriously? You've seen her in action. I don't think she's going to settle down."

"Not right away but in a couple of years she might, once she gets used to being free and starts trusting guys. We can discuss this at home. Let's go there. Please?"

"Don't you have to work?"

"I can go in later. Right now, you, MJ and I have a lot of talking ahead of us. Say yes, I'm begging you. Don't make me call Zoe over here to drag you back."

Daemon looked past her. His color drained.

Zoe lifted her chin in greeting.

He huddled closer to Heather. "You're sure?"

"About what?"

"Us. You and me."

She'd never been certain of anything, except this. She wanted him more than life. "Absolutely. How about you?"

He pulled her to him and kept her there with his fierce hug.

The best answer ever.

Epilogue

Six months later...

Halloween celebrations were going full blast in the French Quarter, making it easy for weres, vamps and other supernaturals to roam the streets and come in for their evening appointments. Tonight, no one questioned how they looked.

Heather ushered triplets, each a vamp, into the largest treatment room. The guys were handsome but pasty. She gestured to blood-filled bottles decorated with jack-o-lanterns or black cats, mortal trappings that were silly but fun. "Enjoy your drinks while you wait. They're on the house tonight."

Halloween was the busiest and most lucrative time for the service, followed by Mardi Gras.

A festive air pulsed through the place along with the usual unearthly noises.

Stoked for a good time, Heather boogied back to her desk that she'd decorated with plastic skulls, cobwebs and rubber spiders.

Zoe had brought in her carrion plant collection to spruce up her space, refusing to decorate it with anything she considered dumb. Heather figured Zoe's perpetual gloomy mood was because she hadn't found anyone yet. Hopefully, she would and soon, too, no matter what she said about not wanting someone to love. Like MJ, Constance played the field. Tonight, she wore orange and black to show her support for the holiday. Becca had donned a witch's pointy hat she'd wear later to a party with Eric.

Heather had gone all out, black lipstick, a black leather cat suit, her pretty mask and thigh-high boots. She's changed from her C cup back to the A she'd once had. Daemon liked her the way she was naturally.

He strode down the hall, clipboard in hand. In addition to his black jeans, tee and cowboy boots, he wore fake horns and a tail as his costume. The tail swished merrily.

He joined her at the desk and offered a sweet kiss. All they could indulge in there since they were both on the clock.

Months ago, Becca had hired Daemon as muscle to help the female staff, except for Zoe. She insisted on going it alone. He wrestled unruly clients to the treatment tables and kept the amorous ones in line. Not only was he a valuable team member, he had purpose now.

Heather brushed her lips over his. "Hungry?"

"Always."

"Open up." She pushed two Hostess cupcakes into his mouth.

He swallowed them whole and released a small belch.

She didn't mind. That's who he was. Uncivilized but fun. Sweet and kind. The only guy for her.

He licked her thumb in thanks.

"Daemon!" A female staffer ran into the hall, her hair and clothes disheveled. "We need you now!"

"Gotta go." He pecked Heather's mouth and sprinted to the treatment room.

MJ left her small office. She'd wanted to wear her leather harness tonight, as she had at the club. Heather and Daemon had nixed that, so she dressed in hot-pink harem pants and a top like the actress on the old series *I Dream of Jeannie*.

"Hey, Precious, need more forms."

Heather gave MJ another stack of legal papers Becca insisted they use for wish releases. MJ granted one small wish to those customers who wanted an extra add-on with their makeover service. Weres who weren't completely finished with their treatments had wished for thick clouds to hide a full moon on the nights they took their ladies out. Vamps wanted a chance to taste food again. Most hadn't liked it as much as blood, but at least they didn't pine for burgers or steaks any longer.

Given the reasonable price for the service, it was a hit, brought in mucho bucks and afforded MJ a nice salary.

"Thanks." She gave Heather a wink and backed toward her office. "Looking forward to the club later."

"Me, too." A mortal club where they'd enjoy drinks and laughter then cut loose, but would stay dressed.

Daemon and MJ had learned nudity wasn't necessary for a great time.

Once Daemon and Heather got home, with MJ arriving after she'd had fun with her hookup, the real party would begin, starring BDSM—Daemon pretending to be a Dom and MJ cheerleading the wanton action.

The perfect setup. Until MJ found her man, they belonged together. They'd surely changed each other in their own way.

Daemon and MJ had freed Heather's wild side while nurturing her inherent sweetness. She'd brought out their tender qualities and their enormous capacities to love even as she craved their wicked ways.

They were family now, hers to protect, help and depend on. What Heather had sought for so many years. What nothing and no one would ever change.

Becca had said be careful what you ask for.

Heather didn't have to any longer. A wish had nothing to do with her life now. Love, friendship and trust were the only magic she'd ever need.

Feeling right with her world, she hummed *We've Only Just Begun* and got back to work.

Want to see more from this author?
Here's a taster for you to enjoy!

Taming the Beast:
Mastering the Beast
Tina Donahue

Excerpt

Zoe stormed toward a treatment room, ready to rumble.

As the top enforcer at From Crud to Stud, *the* New Orleans' makeover service for supernatural beings, she didn't take lip or attitude from anyone. She'd made that fatal mistake in the past. First with hard-nosed villagers during the Salem witch trials, which had been way worse than the fluff shown on the History Channel. Then with Satan after he'd wooed her to Hell using his typical bait-and-switch scheme. What a creep he'd turned out to be.

Twice in her existence, she'd let guys determine her future. No more. She was her own woman now, uninterested in men. Her work here was all she needed, guided by her determination to do things the mortal way—suffer and endure, no supernatural powers allowed.

She pushed open the door and faced a sickly looking vamp who sported a pasty complexion and a man bun. Hardly a babe magnet. Only fierce dedication and hard work would turn him into Mr. Charm. "Yo. On the table. Now." Before the staffers helped him to suppress his inner beast, she had to strap him down. An easy-peasy job for a reformed demon with hardcore ways.

He licked his fangs flirtatiously. Some might say hungrily. "Hey. I'm—"

"I'm not going to ask again."

"Easy, cupcake. I'm just trying to make conversation. What's your name?"

"Kim Kardashian."

"Yeah?" He regarded her scrawny figure. "You changed. Like a lot."

"It's an illusion. Call it my work uniform. Once I'm on my own time, I blossom."

"Cool."

They circled each other, both ready to pounce.

Given his powers, he struck first and sank his teeth into her neck.

She tapped her foot but let him do his thing.

"Gah." He gagged and recoiled. "Damn, you taste like hell."

Surprise, surprise. "Time for you to learn some manners. Good thing you came to us."

He eyed a female staffer strolling by and gave her a toothy grin.

Zoe got in his face. "Park your butt over there now."

"When I'm good and ready, sweetheart." He craned his neck to watch the staffer. "Run along."

Zoe rammed her saddle shoe into his foot and her elbow into his gut, wrestled him to the table then strapped him in so he'd never get free. Not even if he morphed into a freaking bat. His frustrated hiss mingled with a reaper's wail, zombie grunts and were howls.

Lovely sounds, ordinarily. However, tonight something was off, the evening heavy with tension that breathed danger. Similar to when another demon slunk nearby.

Warily, she approached the last two treatment rooms. Both were empty. The walls bore claw marks from former inhabitants.

Maybe she was overreacting due to the calendar date. Halloween approached, the dumbest and most inaccurate holiday ever.

Heather, a healer and the good fairy receptionist there, had decorated her desk with plastic skulls. Fake cobwebs hung from the faux gas fixtures. Rubber spiders stuck to the coral walls and spelled out *Boo!* on the artificial brick floor.

Zoe resisted the urge to roll her eyes or say anything unkind, since Heather was her BFF.

Heather smiled adoringly at Daemon, a former satyr. He'd come to the service more than a year ago to ditch his horns, tail and hooves in order to look fully human so he could boogie with mortal babes. Not only did he work there now as an enforcer, he and Heather had shacked up, their love more enduring than Romeo and Juliet's. They laughed easily and gazed at each other with tenderness and respect whenever they weren't busy making out like sex-starved teens.

Loneliness tightened Zoe's chest. She ached from unexpected longing but shook it off.

Romance wasn't what she needed or could risk. She'd learned that brutal truth centuries ago when she'd had wanted one guy, just one, more than life itself. What a hot mess *that* had turned out to be, especially after she'd sold her soul to get his affection. Talk about false advertising. What she'd ended up with was a one-way ticket to Hell along with Satan's negligent shrug and pissy explanation about what had happened.

"It all boils down to free will." He'd grinned. "The guy doesn't want you. What can I do?"

Satan made first-class louses look like Prince Charming.

However, he had taught her an important lesson. No way would she ever fall for another man and give him her heart, if she'd had one. These past years, she'd sworn off dating, companionship and especially sex even though celibacy was killing her. Especially tonight.

The only thing she couldn't figure out was why.

"Zoe." Becca, another BFF and the half-mortal witch who owned this place, motioned her to the other hall. "Can we have a word in my office?"

That same edgy feeling returned and grew stronger. She expected a demon to pounce from behind the feathery ferns or potted plants that adorned the reception area.

No one was there.

"Now?" Becca led the way. Her harem pants rode low on her voluptuous hips and swished around her legs. Her tie-front crop top hugged her ample boobs. Both garments were iridescent blue that matched her eyes.

In her office, she gestured Zoe to the needlepoint sofa that faced the antique desk. Displayed on the cabinet behind it were numerous photos of Becca and Eric, a minor god she'd met and had fallen in love with when he'd come there for treatment.

Melancholy hit, followed by dread. Zoe worried another staffer had found her man and now that guy was going to work here like Daemon. A new enforcer would cut even deeper into her territory. The only thing she had left.

Rather than sitting, she squared her shoulders prepared to defend her turf.

Becca smiled cautiously. A sure sign she wasn't certain what to do, like when she practiced her witchcraft. Poor thing had been studying hard but managed more misses than hits when she concocted spells or potions. If not for her mom, Rowena, helping with those things, she would have been shit outta luck.

Zoe lifted her chin and got bolder than she felt. "Is this about Constance?"

Another BFF and the resident voodoo priestess here. Given that Constance liked men big time, it was a miracle she hadn't been the first on their team to hook up.

Becca frowned slightly. "What about her?"

"Shouldn't she be in here, too?" Seemed reasonable if she had a once-in-a-lifetime romance to gush about.

"No. She's with a client, removing some of his memories."

Zoe suspected those involved the dude's former girlfriend that Constance wanted him to forget. "So the client is the one she's in love with?"

"Love?" Becca pressed her hand to her chest. "Oh, my God, is she serious about someone? I didn't know she was even dating on a regular basis. What have you heard?"

Confused, Zoe shook her head. "Nothing. Is this about MJ?"

She was a genie who'd used to live in Daemon's ring before he set her free. Currently, she was his and Heather's houseguest and also worked there granting wishes to clients for a price. Like Constance, MJ enjoyed doing the nasty with guys. Little wonder she'd found her man. "She's hooked up with someone?"

"You mean permanently?" Becca's eyes widened. The heavy black makeup surrounding them made them appear larger against her fair skin. "I don't think so.

Daemon had to separate her and a were earlier. They were really going at it. Once she left him, she had her eye on a warlock. Have you heard or seen something different?"

"Uh-uh. I thought you knew something and wanted to tell me about it in here."

"Oh…no." She made a face and shook it off. "This is about business. We've been really swamped this year, so I've decided to expand. I've already talked to the building's owner about taking over the entire floor and renovating it for our use."

Zoe's tension drained away. "Cool. You want me to keep the workers in line in between my other stuff?" She slammed her fist against her palm. "I'll be happy to."

Becca stopped fingering her short red hair. "I don't want you to kill yourself by working so hard."

"How could I do that?" She frowned. "I'm already dead, not to mention immortal."

"That's not what I meant." Becca waved her hand dismissively. "I want you to enjoy your work."

That funny feeling returned and made Zoe queasy. "Who says I don't like what I do here? Oh, hey, is this about Daemon horning in on more of my stuff? Uh-uh. He's already keeping the clients in line for the other staff. I don't need him to do that for me. I'm capable. Hell, I'm a better enforcer than him. I do not want him anywhere near my customers."

"No problem. He won't be." Becca cleared her throat. "Stefin, Anatol and Taro will be here for that from now on."

Footfalls rang in the hall.

Three guys strode into Becca's office, their movements fluid and assured. Each looked thirty or so, in mortal years, and had dressed in black, their shirts silk, their boots and pants elegant, like bouncers wear at an elite club.

No one was dancing in here, especially Zoe.

A faint sulfur scent emanated from the unholy trio. Flames flared briefly in their eyes.

Demons. The trouble she'd sensed earlier.

She froze, too stunned to move or speak.

The guy in the middle was easily six-three and nicely muscular, his blond hair shoulder-length. His rough good looks, bronze complexion and stubble put the va-va-voom in virile. Sin filled his light gray eyes, his mood dangerous and predatory.

Her belly fluttered.

He winked.

Disquiet and lust rolled through Zoe. Her legs went watery.

The guy on the right proved equally tall and powerfully built. Beautiful, he had rich-chocolate skin, dark eyes and long hair worn in dreadlocks.

Those babies would feel awesome gliding across her naked boobs and thighs — until he screwed her over like every other male had done.

She steeled herself against his allure.

He smiled.

A freaking dimple dented his right cheek, his grin an unusual combination of boyish mischief and raw sensuality.

Her pussy creamed.

Hot didn't begin to describe the last guy's masculine features, deep-blue eyes and thick auburn hair. Those wavy locks trailed past his ears and curled on his neck. His stubble called to everything female within Zoe, as did his height, big body and the assured way he regarded her.

The guys' enticing sulfur odor enhanced their musky scents, making the mixture wanton and unashamed. Their impressive cocks pushed against their flies.

She bet each of their rods jutted from blond, black or auburn curls.

The room spun.

"Guys." Becca lifted her reddish eyebrows. "This is Zoe."

The introduction seemed to come from far away, Becca's voice muted by the ringing in Zoe's ears. She tried to respond but only managed an odd noise, part grunt, mostly a groan.

Becca edged closer. "Zoe, this is Anatol." She gestured to the black hunk with the dimple. "Stefin." The blond god in the middle winked again. "And Taro." The blue-eyed hottie regarded her intensely. "They're our new enforcers."

Each looked in charge already, their stances saying they wouldn't budge one damn inch for anyone, especially a female demon.

Becca offered a nervous smile. "You'll be working with them from now on."

Working with or for, as in taking orders, yearning helplessly then losing out as she had with the last man in her life?

Like hell.

Home of Erotic Romance

Sign up for our newsletter and find out about all our romance book releases, eBook sales and promotions, sneak peeks and FREE romance books!

About the Author

Tina is an Amazon and international bestselling novelist who writes passionate romance for every taste–'heat with heart'–for traditional publishers and indie. Booklist, Publisher's Weekly, Romantic Times and numerous online sites have praised her work. She's won Readers' Choice Awards, was named a finalist in the EPIC competition, received a Book of the Year award, The Golden Nib Award, awards of merit in the RWA Holt Medallion competitions, and second place in the NEC RWA contests. She's featured in the Novel & Short Story Writer's Market. Before penning romances, she worked at a major Hollywood production company in Story Direction.

Tina loves to hear from readers. You can find her contact information, website details and author profile page at https://www.totallybound.com